A concussive wave of heat swept over them, carrying them several feet through the air before they hit the concrete and rolled to a stop against the wheel of a truck.

Every point of her body was bruised or numb from the crashing fall. Knuckles, elbows, knees, heels. Ivan's full weight on top of her made it hard to breathe. But even as her lungs protested and her vision spun in circles, Carly clamped her hands around his biceps, trying to reverse their positions and drag him behind the shelter of the pillar.

But in the next second, Ivan shifted, bracing his elbows on either side of her and palming her head, tucking her face against his chest and shielding her body with his as flying metal and burning car parts rained down around them.

A heavy chunk of twisted fender clanged down beside them. Carly shoved at his chest, hating the vulnerability of his position. Instead of budging, his hold on her tightened. "Damn it, Ivan. *I* protect *you*!"

He jerked once, and she knew he'd been hit.

PERSONAL PROTECTION

USA TODAY Bestselling Author
JULIE MILLER

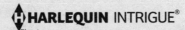

HARLEQUIN INTRIGUE®

For Jana Boyll Thompson, my singing buddy.

I so enjoy hanging out with you at City Singers and doing a show together every now and then. We'll try not to get into too much trouble.

ISBN-13: 978-1-335-60455-2

Personal Protection

Copyright © 2019 by Julie Miller

PLEASE RECYCLE
THIS PRODUCT IS RECYCLABLE

Recycling programs for this product may not exist in your area.

HARLEQUIN®
™ www.Harlequin.com

Printed in U.S.A.

Julie Miller is an award-winning *USA TODAY* bestselling author of breathtaking romantic suspense—with a National Readers' Choice Award and a Daphne du Maurier Award, among other prizes. She has also earned an *RT Book Reviews* Career Achievement Award. For a complete list of her books, monthly newsletter and more, go to juliemiller.org.

Books by Julie Miller

Harlequin Intrigue

Rescued by the Marine
Do-or-Die Bridesmaid
Personal Protection

The Precinct

Beauty and the Badge
Takedown
KCPD Protector
Crossfire Christmas
Military Grade Mistletoe
Kansas City Cop

The Precinct: Bachelors in Blue

APB: Baby
Kansas City Countdown
Necessary Action
Protection Detail

The Precinct: Cold Case

Kansas City Cover-Up
Kansas City Secrets
Kansas City Confessions

Visit the Author Profile page at Harlequin.com.

CAST OF CHARACTERS

Prince Ivan Mostek of Lukinburg—The crown prince is ending government corruption and bringing his country into the modern world. But not everyone likes change. Someone has already tried to kill him and blow up half a city to stop him. When he travels to Kansas City on a trade mission, he discovers that the biggest threat is within his own entourage. With no one to trust, he turns to an outsider—a tough, sexy KCPD cop—for protection.

Officer Carly Valentine—Masquerading as Prince Ivan's American girlfriend requires a Cinderella makeover for this kick-ass undercover cop. Bodyguard duty doesn't faze her. Neither does ferreting out the traitor in their midst. But embracing her feminine side and falling in love with the mysterious prince means risking her heart. She's working class and he's royalty. Even if they survive the attempts on his life, how can they ever have a happily-ever-after?

Joe Hendricks—Carly's precinct captain is working as her handler on this undercover operation.

Aleksandr Petrovic—Prince Ivan's friend and trusted adviser. But can anyone really be trusted under the circumstances?

Filip Milevski—Prince Ivan's chief of security. Is this longtime servant to the crown past his prime?

Eduard Nagy—The newest member of the prince's security team is eager to please.

Danya Pavluk—The prince's by-the-book bodyguard has an attitude.

Galina Honchar—The prince's chief of staff is organized and efficient.

Ralph Decker—A reporter for the *Kansas City Journal*. Just what kind of story is he after?

Prologue

May 1—Lukinburg Day in St. Feodor, on the steps of the historic palace square

"In three months, St. Feodor will play host to a group of dignitaries from our sister city in the United States. We will introduce the Americans to the charm of our country and show them that they need us as much as we need them. They need our rugged mountains, our beautiful beaches, our vast supply of natural resources, the skills and grace of our people."

Cameras flashed in the crowd, and the low white noise of television and radio commentators from across Europe and the United States, speaking a dozen different languages, buzzed in the background beneath static from the old broadcasting system. The world was waiting for tiny, mountainous Lukinburg in Eastern Europe to blossom after decades of oppression to take its rightful place on the world stage once more.

A black-haired woman in a cream-colored suit moved in behind the prince at the podium and tapped him on the shoulder. "Do not forget to mention the city's name, Your Highness," she reminded him.

"Thank you, Galina," the prince whispered before turning back to the microphone. "Kansas City, Missouri, our sister city, will become Lukinburg's partner in worldwide respect and future prosperity. We shall be great friends."

The crowd erupted in applause. He adjusted his glasses at his temple and scanned the throng of onlookers through the bulletproof glass surrounding the podium. He looked past the placards here to support the new regime to the handful of scowling doubters with their own less supportive signs, waiting for the opportune moment to voice a protest.

A public gathering of this size in the capital on one of the country's biggest holidays once would have been a prime target for dissidents. Change was hard for any citizen. Change was the enemy to those who'd once held positions of power, who were now either imprisoned or being asked to embrace what was good for the country over what was lucrative for themselves. But the prince had reached out to those dissidents, had listened to their complaints and fears, had formed alliances and reached compromises with many of them. Yet, some of the most die-hard rebels hadn't given up the fight, and they would always see the new monarchy as their enemy.

Lukinburg's army had some of the finest trained soldiers in the world, and the plainclothes security force that now surrounded the country's leaders at every venue were on constant guard against any threat that would topple the fragile new government. He looked at his friends and former military comrades flanking him on the podium. They were doing this. They were making Lukinburg great again. Their hard work and dedication had given the country reason to celebrate today.

Ivan Mostek, the crown prince of Lukinburg, was nearing the end of his long fight to replace the corrupt government of this country. A hardworking regency government and brave voters had replaced the corrupt dictator and mafia-like power brokers who had made Lukinburg a haven for criminals and arms trafficking. Part of electing a new Parliament and reestablishing the democratic monarchy this picturesque country had enjoyed before World War II was locating a true heir to the Lukinburg throne. As a distant cousin of the last legitimate king's late grandnephew, that dubious honor fell to Ivan. Plucked from graduate school where he'd been earning his MBA, he'd accepted the position. Patriotism and DNA had left him with no other choice but to say yes, and accept that within the next year, he would be crowned king.

With the discovery of gold and mica deep beneath the mountains east of Lake Feodor, Lukinburg now had raw materials that countries in the West and Far East were clamoring to build their electronics and develop new computer technologies. The prince had implemented environmentally safe mining practices to sustain the new resources. From his newfound position of power, he was jump-starting the country's economy, feeding the poor, capitalizing on new industries and putting people to work—all while paying tribute to Lukinburg's traditional culture and storied history.

Public appearances were necessary to assure the citizens of the solidity of the new government. And public appearances meant crowds of people and noisy fanfare and making speeches. After the cheers had died down, he continued, "Kansas City's manufacturing, agricultural and business leaders will be in our beautiful country, in this fair city, in three weeks. A carefully chosen delegation of representatives from Lukinburg will negotiate trade agreements and cultural exchanges that will benefit both our countries."

He spied movement in the shadows of the pointed Gothic archways in the cathedral across from the palace steps where he stood. He looked across the podium to his friend Konrad Pavluk. They exchanged a nod of awareness. Konrad had spotted the movement, too. The other man drifted across the dais to stand beside Galina. Anyone less observant would have missed the hidden squeeze of hands, the subtle whisper of a warning. She nodded and moved up behind the prince again to relay a message.

The military marksmen stationed in decorative ramparts atop the stone buildings surrounding the public square didn't seem concerned by the hooded man in the long coat making his way through the crowd of bystanders. Maybe they didn't see him. Or perhaps, as the prince had confided to his best friend only days earlier, someone within his inner circle was still working with the extremists. Did the uniformed guards' lack of response mean they were unobservant? Traitors? Was he overly paranoid about the prince's safety because an attempt had already been made on his life?

Although that sniper had been captured and taken into custody, the threats against Ivan's life continued. It had been random gunfire that had wounded his driver and ignited the engine of the car they'd taken to an ore refinement facility being built outside the city. Were the extremists here today? Mingling with this crowd of innocent civilians? Would they strike again, regardless of the casualties a group this big might sustain? Was the man in the hooded coat one of them?

He glanced over to the security chief, Filip Milevski. Although the dark glasses he wore made the direction of his gaze unreadable, the stocky man with salt-and-pepper hair was on the radio pinned to his wrist, no doubt asking for a situation update from his men and hopefully sounding a potential alert to stop the man who was now circling the fountain in the middle of the square.

The prince's voice was slightly less composed, tinged with a bit of anger, when he continued. "I promise to make Lukinburg great again. We will move past the shame of our former leaders. We will return to the democratic monarchy of our ancestors. I will work closely with the new prime minister and your votes will count. All your votes," he added, perhaps emphasizing to the extremists in the audience that they were not excluded from the new government.

Another round of cheers from the crowd nearly drowned out a lone dissenter who booed him. "You're selling us out, Ivan!"

Security Chief Milevski sidled closer to the prince. "Wrap it up, Your Highness." He moved Konrad and another one of his men farther down the granite steps in front of the podium. "There are too many of us exposed here. We're all in danger."

His gaze zeroed in on the hooded man. He'd sat on the edge of the fountain and was unbuttoning his long coat. The prince kept talking into the microphone, keeping the crowd engaged while members of the security team made their way through the onlookers to reach the suspect. "We need free trade. Our people need food."

"Our people need a leader they can respect!" The protest came from another corner of the audience.

"I agree. For too long, we have been led by men our people fear. Fear doesn't put food in people's bellies. Our people are working again. They aren't afraid to leave their homes and share their opinions and vote however they please."

A tall man, with hair as black at the prince's himself, moved in beside him with a whispered warning. "Your Highness. We need to go."

The security team converged on the fountain as the hooded man stood. "End Ivan!"

"Bomb!"

There were too many screams to make out the words that followed. The crowd split and ran like a tidal surge away from the fountain.

"Stop him!"

"Save the prince!"

Armed men in suits ran forward.

A sniper guarding the gathering from a turret high above the street raised his rifle and took aim at the insurgent. But he was too late.

"Save yourselves!" Prince Ivan warned. His bodyguards swarmed around him and shoved him to the stone steps behind the podium. The square erupted with light and the deafening roar of an explosion.

The prince's cheek scraped against stone as the black-haired man covered his body with his. His ears were stopped up by the concussive blast. But he heard the screams of his people, the stampede of running feet, gunfire, as if the violence was all happening far in the distance instead of a mere few yards beyond the podium.

He spotted blood on the steps a split second before something sharp and hot seared his skin, cutting through the invisible target on his back.

The prince's public rallying speech in the heart of Lukinburg's capital left him wounded. Landmarks had been damaged. People were injured, dead.

The dignitaries from Kansas City wouldn't be coming.

Chapter One

After the explosion in the palace square, the business-people and government officials Ivan Mostek needed to talk to in Kansas City had refused to travel to Lukinburg. They were concerned for their safety, and rightly so. The shrapnel scars on his back were still pink and tender from that attack.

But he wouldn't give up on the new government's vision to reform his country.

So, the prince had come to Kansas City. These negotiations were going to happen, no matter what a few leftovers from the old regime thought of him. They'd lost their power and weren't above using an assassination to get it back. Perhaps the threats he faced were coming from loyalists who believed the modernization of their country would irrevocably change it, and they'd lose their cultural identity. What they'd lose was any kind of standing as a first world country. Their economy was dying, and the old ways didn't feed his people.

Ivan Mostek, Crown Prince of Lukinburg, the symbolic leader of his country and heir to the throne, had no intention of giving power back to the thugs that had nearly ruined their country, nor did he intend to destroy any of the things that made Lukinburg so uniquely special. The plan was a good one. But he had to survive first. Survive this trip to the States. Survive until his coronation and hopefully live a long and healthy life afterward as the leader of Lukinburg.

The first step in that plan meant leaving his country and traveling to Kansas City for a week. The second step meant surrounding himself with people he trusted. That was proving more of a challenge than he'd expected since it seemed that no matter what security measures his team put into place, the threats kept coming. So, he'd put in a call to KCPD to ask for help from strangers. The local police had no ties to Lukinburg. He was counting on them to provide a layer of protection that couldn't be influenced by politics, fear of change or revenge.

Striding up the steps from his limousine, Ivan followed his chief of security, Filip Milevski, into the lobby of Fourth Precinct headquarters. His trusted adviser and good friend, Aleksandr Petrovic, followed right behind him, while another bodyguard, Danya Pavluk, brought up the rear. His third bodyguard and new driver, Eduard Nagy, would park the car and wait for them to finish their respective meetings.

After lining up their visitor badges, Filip, a tall, beefy man with graying sideburns, punched the button to call the elevator. "I will escort you to your meeting with Captain Hendricks. Then Danya and I will meet with the SWAT captain and senior patrol officer to co-ordinate security at your public appearances."

Ivan smoothed the knot of his tie and nodded. "Do not forget to have them set up extra officers outside the Lukinburg embassy on Saturday. Your team can work with embassy security inside, but the ball will dramatically increase traffic and bring many wealthy and important local and state people to that part of town."

"I forget nothing," Filip huffed, as though it was an insult to remind him. The elevator doors opened, and he waited for the car to empty before leading them inside. "I do not understand why you could not stay at the hotel and let me handle the police department. This Joe Hendricks you are meeting with is not on my list of contacts." No, but Chief of Police Taylor had recommended the precinct captain when Ivan had called to ask for the secret favor. "I cannot control your safety when you surprise me with meetings that are not on your agenda."

Ah, yes. Filip loved his routines. If he had any idea what Ivan was planning behind his back, he'd be livid.

"I told you, this is personal. You do not need to be involved."

"But it is my responsibility—"

"I am inside a police station. I will be fine without you hovering over me." He grinned at Aleks, who was people watching the comings and goings of officers, detectives, visitors and staff through the lobby checkpoint and service counters. He flicked his friend's arm to get his attention. "You should have brought a camera," he teased.

Aleks's grin formed a bright crescent of white in his long black beard. "Did you see that plaque on the wall? They have created a memorial to a little girl—"

"Aleks…" Ivan urged his friend to join them. "Business first. Sightseeing later. You know we must—"

"Hold that elevator!"

Ivan's sentence trailed off and he instinctively grabbed the door as a woman with a dirty, soot-streaked blond ponytail darted onto the elevator. She pulled in an equally grimy, handcuffed man by his upper arm and guided him to the corner farthest away from Ivan and his staff, ordering her captive to face the wall. Filip cursed under his breath as he and Danya quickly positioned themselves between Ivan and their guests and allowed the doors to close.

"Thanks." He saw the woman wore fingerless gloves when she pushed some flyaway strands of hair off her face. He also saw the badge hanging from a chain around her neck. Ivan's senses tingled with an alertness he had to hide. "Sorry. I didn't relish dragging this dirtbag up the stairs or waiting for the next elevator."

She wore a long, dusty man's coat over jeans and worn leather boots that were nearly as big as his own feet. Gloves? Coat? Boots?

In August?

No wonder there was a sheen of perspiration on her pink cheeks.

As intrigued by her apparent toughness as he was curious about her ratty, overheated appearance, he offered her a succinct nod. "We are happy to oblige the local constabulary."

Her prisoner glanced over his shoulder at Ivan. "What's that mean?"

"Quiet." The officer nodded toward the keypad and asked Filip to push the button for her. "Third floor, please."

"We should not share an elevator, Your High—"

"This is fine," Ivan insisted, reaching around his security chief to press the number three button himself. It was probably best not to advertise his real identity just yet. Not until all his security was in place. "We are here to make friends with the people of Kansas City, not make their lives more difficult."

"You talk funny," the handcuffed man slurred, laughing at their accents.

And he smelled funny. Dreadful, actually, as Ivan crinkled his nose up against the odors of urine, body odor and smoke filling the confined space. At least, he hoped it was the criminal and not the female officer escorting him who reeked of the streets. Ivan had been trained to keep such negative observations to himself and be a polite gentleman at all times. "English is not my first language."

"Your English is better than mine, pal."

"Dougie. Sorry about that, sir." The woman jerked on the handcuffs, warning her prisoner to be quiet again. Apparently, standing still and keeping his mouth shut was an ongoing battle for the twitchy bum. "I am already in a mood. Don't push it."

Even though the woman wasn't terribly chatty, Ivan noted that she was extremely observant. She marked their number and position on the elevator as it began

its ascent. She sized up the flak vest and guns Filip and
Danya wore beneath their suit jackets and pulled back
the front of her coat to keep her gun within easy reach.
Although he wanted to reassure the woman that they
meant her no harm, backing up that claim would mean
that he'd have to identify himself and his entourage.
And Ivan wasn't ready to reveal anything when he had
this much of an audience surrounding him.

His training in the Lukin military had made him
observant, too. The woman had an ordinary face. She
was of average height and indeterminate shape, thanks
to the bulky coat she wore. In addition to a stylist, she
needed a comb and a shower and a much more coop-
erative prisoner. Ivan curled his fingers into his palms,
fighting back the urge to push Filip and Danya aside
and assist her with the recalcitrant man who muttered
and fidgeted instead of obeying her authority. Maybe
a good twenty years older and hundred pounds heavier
than her, the man seemed familiar with handcuffs and
causing trouble. No wonder she'd been anxious to get
him into a jail cell or interview room and off her hands.

He also noticed she had green eyes.

And lips. Ivan averted his gaze as if he'd uttered that
ridiculous observation out loud. Of course, she had
lips. But they had drawn his attention to the middle of
her flushed face. Despite her determined lack of fem-
ininity, her lips were pink and asymmetrical, sleekly
defined on top and decadently full on the bottom. She
had a mouth that reminded him just how delightful it
was to kiss a willing woman, and just how long he'd
denied himself that pleasure.

"Y'all ain't cops, are ya?" Her prisoner twisted around again, ignoring her order to face the wall. "With your fancy suits and fancy accents. Damn foreigners."

"Douglas Freeland," she warned. "You be nice to these people."

"I ain't been nothin' but nice this morning. I got a sickness and you know it. You set me up." He called her a crude name that fisted Ivan's hands with the need to shut him up and make him apologize. He was embarrassed to see his bodyguards ignoring the verbal abuse and staring fixedly at the elevator doors as they slowed to a stop. "I ain't goin' back in."

The moment the doors slid open, the prisoner twisted out of her grasp. In the next second, he spun around and butted his fat, bald head against her more delicate skull.

The urge to intervene jolted through Ivan's legs as she tumbled to the floor. But Filip and Danya pushed him against the railing, blocking him from the scuffle. "Protect the prince!"

Not that the officer apparently needed his or anyone's help. Before the man got both feet off the elevator, her legs shot out and she tripped him. Then she was on top of the guy with a feral yell as she smushed her attacker's face to the floor. Several other officers from the third floor had rushed to help, but they stopped in their tracks, backing up a step as she hauled the prisoner to his feet. The big man wasn't muttering anymore. She pushed him against the seam between the wall and the elevator, using him to prop the door open while she checked his cuffs and evened out her breathing.

Filip took Ivan by the arm to lead him off the elevator. But Ivan didn't need to be sandwiched between his bodyguards. The woman, despite the blow to the head, seemed to have the situation under control.

Still, he knew the toll hand-to-hand combat like that could take on a person. There would be bruises, and her head would be throbbing. He shrugged free of Filip's grip. "Are you all right, miss?"

"Officer. Officer Valentine." Her green eyes widened with a message that could be understood in any language. *Get off the damn elevator already and let me do my job.*

"Very well. Gentlemen." They all exited the elevator and headed to the sergeant's desk for directions to the captain's office.

With a nod to the officers who'd come to her aid, Officer Valentine pushed a long tendril of caramel-colored hair off her face and walked her prisoner through the maze of desks on the main floor. Her dialogue trailed off as they went their separate ways. "That was your big plan? Escape onto a floor filled with cops? Now I get to add a second assault charge..."

Relief that Officer Valentine was all right, as well as admiration at how she'd handled the situation herself, eased the tension inside him. Ivan wondered at the rush of adrenaline he felt ebbing from his system and chalked it up to jet lag finally catching up with him.

"THIS IS EVERYTHING on my schedule while I am here in Kansas City." Ivan forwarded the text from his chief of staff, Galina Honchar, to Captain Hendricks's phone.

In turn, Joe Hendricks, the captain of the Fourth Precinct, copied the list of events and locations to his administrative assistant in the adjoining office and asked her to make a printout. "Occasionally, a meeting runs long or something unexpected comes up…"

"Last-minute changes could be handled by the liaison officer you're asking for," the captain finished. "She'll be able to keep me in loop, so I can have whatever assistance is needed on standby."

That was part of his plan, Ivan conceded. "That would be a benefit to your department." But he was asking for something more than a communications liaison with the local police.

After sending Filip and Danya off to their respective meetings, the only person from Lukinburg here with Ivan on the third floor was Aleksandr Petrovic. Last he'd seen, Aleks was cooling his heels in Captain Hendricks's outer office, chatting up the captain's administrative assistant. Even though the woman wore a wedding ring and was obviously pregnant, flirting and having a good time seemed to be hardwired into Aleks's DNA. He had survived the mines and poverty of Moravska, relying on hard work and sheer determination to leave his past behind him. His friend had been a city kid, raised in a modest neighborhood in St. Feodor, and had used that innate charm to impress the right people and negotiate one successful business deal after another. To look at them now, with their tailored suits and limousines, Ivan and Aleks seemed to be cut from the same cloth, but their personalities and backgrounds couldn't be more different. Still, Aleks was the one confidant the prince had trusted with the real goal of this meeting, and, if he wasn't too distracted by the woman out there, was keeping an eye out for when Milevski and the rest of the security team returned.

Ivan was learning that secrecy was practically impossible for royalty. But that secrecy was necessary. The crumpled note sitting like a fishing weight in his pocket warned him that keeping his secrets was a matter of life-and-death. "I told my security chief that I have reconnected with an old flame in the US from my military days, when we did joint operations with other countries. That is why I am making this request privately. They believe I am being discreet for romance's sake, not because I suspect a breach among the members of my entourage."

The black man with the weathered face and receding hairline nodded. "I can help you with your request to place an undercover operative inside your delegation for the duration of your visit. I've lined up a couple of candidates of the appropriate age for you to meet."

Ivan reminded him why he sought him out for assistance. "Finding a woman who served in the military is the only plausible way I could think of for me to have met an American and have had the time to develop a relationship with her. I worked with several American soldiers when I was in the military police."

"I haven't told them why they've been summoned to my office yet. I have to admit, this feels a bit like I'm playing matchmaker."

"I assure you, that is not the case, Captain." A tinge of awkwardness heated his skin. "I do not like that I have been forced into this situation. But I must choose a woman today, before I leave this building. My people must get used to seeing her with me. Masquerading as my...paramour...is the only way I can guarantee that we will have time alone to discuss who wants to kill me and devise strategy to unmask the traitor or traitors before they do me or anyone else harm. If I simply take on an American bodyguard, my security team will expect to be working together with that person. Since I do not know who I can trust, I require an ally who reports only to me, one who can convincingly play the role of consort to a prince, and whose qualities meet the needs of this very delicate investigation. I do not care what she looks like or if she fits some profile I would put on a dating site. She only needs to be good at her job."

"That's what I needed to hear." Hendricks pressed a sturdy index finger into the blotter on his desk, the gesture making Ivan think that warning finger would be pressed against his chest—royalty or not—if he dared to misuse one of Hendricks's officers. "If I hear that anything freaky happens to my officer while she's working with you, I promise I will bring the full force of this department down on your head."

"Understood. A good officer protects his troops. I respect that. And I will respect her."

Hendricks nodded. "Then let's do this, Your Highness."

Ignoring the urge to rub at the tension cording the back of his neck, Ivan nodded his appreciation. He was still getting used to answering to *prince* and *Your*

Highness, although the proud posture and cautious, controlled movements that had been drilled into him during his stint in the military and on a UN coalition team in Bosnia served him well in conveying the air of authority he needed to project. The suit and tie he wore were better fitted and more expensive than the clothes he'd worn when he'd been a happy, anonymous commoner. He'd put on the hand-me-downs he'd worn growing up in the poor mountain village where his aunt and uncle had raised him if it meant he could go back to being an ordinary guy without the death threats and suspicions about the people closest to him churning inside his brain. He'd trade his penthouse suite for his old studio apartment in Moravska if it meant he'd no longer have the future of an entire country resting on his shoulders.

But those shoulders were broad and strong from the years he'd worked in the mines. The military had disciplined him, and a technology degree had given him a better life. He would do whatever was necessary to save the fledgling monarchy and put the discontents who would bring their country to its knees again out of business forever. Saving his own skin would be an added bonus.

He adjusted the glasses that pinched his nose and looked across the desk into Joe Hendricks's golden-brown eyes. "You understand my need for secrecy?"

"I do." The man with the salt-and-pepper hair that receded into twin points atop his coffee-colored skin leaned back in his chair. "The fewer people who know about this charade, the better. Only you, me and the officer you select will know exactly what's going on. I'll serve as her undercover handler on this assignment." He rose from his chair and crossed to a set of blinds and opened them, revealing a bank of windows that overlooked a hallway and a beehive of desks and cubicle walls beyond that where uniformed officers, detectives, administrative staff and even a couple of criminals handcuffed to their chairs—including the lowlife who had attacked Officer Valentine—worked or waited. "If there's any chance the threat is legit, and one of those people—what did you call them?"

"They call themselves Lukin Loyalists. I call them the remnants of the mafia thugs who used to control our government. Lukin is a nickname we gave the citizens who were part of the underground resistance during World War II. These people are nothing like those brave souls."

"I thought I heard on the news a while back that the Loyalist situation had been resolved."

"So we thought." Ivan inhaled a deep breath and slowly released his frustration with the entire situation. "There are still some philosophical disagreements, but we've given them a voice in the new government. The minority whip in our Parliament is a Loyalist. He denounced the assassination attempt in the capital."

"There could be some fringe members of the party who feel their leadership has sold them out."

"Seven people died in that blast in St. Feodor, including a friend of mine. Whoever these people are, I take their threats seriously."

Hendricks agreed. "If one or more of these Loyalists

are in Kansas City, planning an assassination attempt, then I want to know about it. I want to prevent any attack if possible and minimalize casualties—including you and my officer."

He pointed through the blinds to two female officers, one wearing a crisp blue uniform. She was engaged in an animated conversation with Aleks. Ivan grinned. Leave it to his friend to find someone new to practice his charms on. It was hard to remember a time when he'd been that carefree and able to stay squarely in a happy moment to enjoy it to the fullest.

The two of them looked very much alike, both with jet-black hair and blue eyes behind the glasses they each wore. Although Ivan stood half an inch taller, Aleks packed more muscle onto his frame. As the prince, he wore his hair cropped military short and kept his beard trimmed close to the angles of his jawline while his friend took his curly facial hair to a shaggy professor look. They'd done their requisite two-year stint in the army after university, where they'd met and become friends. After that, their paths had diverged— one remaining in the military, and the other going back to graduate school—until they'd come together again in service to the new government. They shared looks, history, pride in their country. And yet, the prince's world was vastly different from that of Aleksandr Petrovic. The orphan and the prince. The charmer and the disciplined soldier. Ivan's jaw clenched as his smile faded. Had he sentenced himself to a life of loneliness by answering the call of duty and giving himself over to the needs of his country and its people?

Ivan studied the female officer as she laughed at something Aleks said, and he felt a stab of envy at the normalcy of their interaction. But he reminded himself of the reason why he was here—to find a bodyguard he could trust without question, and an investigator who could help him identify the traitor in his inner circle. Knowing Filip Milevski and the rest of his security detail would be returning in the next fifteen to twenty minutes, Ivan rose, buttoned his jacket and joined Captain Hendricks at the window. He needed to evaluate the officers' suitability for the assignment before selecting his undercover partner.

The uniformed officer sat in one of the chairs lining the hallway, while Aleks stood beside her holding a paper cup of coffee. She touched her hair and ate up Aleks's attention. She was light, fun, perhaps not a strong enough presence to portray a convincing royal consort.

Meanwhile, the other woman, probably a detective, judging by her gray slacks and jacket, was plugged into her earbuds, and was scrolling through information on her phone as she paced the hallway outside the office's glass windows. Her expression remained stern as the uniformed officer caught her attention and tried to share the joke with her. The detective shook her head and continued her pacing. The woman's gravitas would certainly come through as they made their public appearances. She'd be a beauty if she smiled. But the tight lock of her mouth indicated a rigidity that might make it hard for her to adapt to the spontaneous opportunities for secret conversations he expected to arise as the investigation unfolded. And thus far, not much about being a prince was going according to any organized plan.

Captain Hendricks buried his hands in his pockets. "Either one of those women would make a fine liaison officer between you and KCPD."

They were both no doubt competent law enforcement officers, although neither type initially appealed to him. Not the way Officer Valentine's earthy vitality and tempting mouth had switched on his male radar. However, he wasn't here to meet the love of his life. If the woman could act her part as half of a convincing couple, then so could he. His life and the future of his country might depend on making the right choice here. A lightweight or a hard case. "They both have undercover experience?"

"Yes. Detective Wardyn is a few years past her last UC assignment, but she's a seasoned investigator. Officer Rangel is fairly new, but she has a higher marksmanship score."

Brains or brawn? He needed both.

"Then I suppose we should bring them in for a conversation. I don't want to reveal too much to either of them. The fewer people who know the specific details…"

And then a dusty ponytail and long black coat came into view as Officer Valentine shot up from her chair and circled her desk to point her finger in the face of the fat man who was mouthing off at her.

"Tell me more about her." Ivan nodded toward the argument that was not ending well for the handcuffed man. The grungy woman slapped a photograph on the desk in front of the man and forced him to look at it.

"Officer Valentine?" The captain chuckled at something Ivan failed to understand. "Looks like she's brought in a perp for processing."

Perp. Perpetrator. Ivan quickly translated the American slang and determined that Officer Valentine was a brave woman. The man she'd handcuffed made two of her, even with the heavy coat she wore. And yet she...

Ivan felt the hint of a smile relaxing the tight lines beside his mouth. "What about her? Does she have a military background? Earlier, she used a move on her prisoner that I learned during hand-to-hand combat training. Skills like that might be more useful than marksmanship when it comes to a protection detail."

"Carly Valentine? You think *she* can be your princess? Or, you know, personal bodyguard?" Hendricks didn't seem to be a man who was used to stuttering over his words, and he quickly shook off his surprise at Ivan's interest in the woman. "Valentine does a lot of UC work for us. She's a natural on the streets but—"

"Can she look professional when she is not in that costume?" Ivan paused for a moment, wondering if he should trust logic over what his instincts were telling him. "That *is* a costume, yes?"

"Let's hope so. You want to meet her?"

"Yes. There is something about her that seems like we could have worked together before. Under different circumstances. It might make our cover story more believable."

"It's your call." The captain crossed to his desk and picked up the phone to call his assistant. "Brooke? I need to see Carly Valentine in my office ASAP. And pull up her personnel file for me, please. Thanks."

Ivan was still at the window, watching as Carly Valentine answered the phone at her desk. Her shoulders sagged before she glanced back toward the captain's office. She spoke to the man sitting at the desk across from hers. After he nodded, she unlocked the perp from his chair and handed him off to the other officer, who led the prisoner out of sight down a long hallway.

Officer Valentine brushed off the sleeves of the oversize coat she wore, sending up a puff of gray dust in a cloud around her. The shake of her head told Ivan she was nervous about being summoned to the captain's office. She tried to tuck the loose waves back into her ponytail but stopped to inspect her hands. Another officer pointed to her face and Ivan could read the curse on her lips at the streak of soot her fingers had left there. She peeled off her fingerless gloves, quickly wiped her hands and face on a wad of tissues, and then steeled her shoulders before crossing to the captain's outer office. Her coat billowed out around her like the dusters cowboys wore in the American Western movies he loved to watch.

Joe Hendricks stood at his desk, reading information off the computer screen. "I've got Valentine's file here. She did have MP training in the National Guard. Looks like her stint with them ended earlier this year about the same time she earned her associate degree in criminal justice studies. She's been with the department four years. That's not as much experience as either of those officers in the hallway."

Didn't matter. "What does she do for you?"

"Right now, she's working an undercover assignment. She's attached to our human trafficking task force."

"Human trafficking? As in prostitution? Sex slavery?"

Hendricks nodded. "She's on the streets, identifying runaways and at-risk individuals."

Ivan turned back to the window. "And the man she brought in?"

"I'm not sure. But with Valentine, I'm guessing she caught him with his hands on the wrong person. She's a natural-born protector. Can't imagine what kind of fierce mama bear she'd make if she ever decides to have kids."

"Fierce mama bear?" She was in the hallway right outside the office now. Her gaze met and held his through the window. Her eyes were green like the mountain meadows of his homeland—and narrowed with suspicion.

"That's our Valentine."

She blinked, breaking the momentary connection between them. Oblivious to Aleks's curious interest as she walked past him and the other two female officers, she tossed her long ponytail down the center of her back and strode into the assistant's office.

Grimy. Plain. Fierce. Intriguing. Very good at playing her part.

A woman he just might have something in common with.

Chapter Two

"Hey, Brooke." Carly Valentine closed the door behind her and crossed the small office over to her friend's desk. Her pulse thrummed in her ears with more nerves than the adrenaline charge that had raised her heart rate when Dougie Freeland had whacked her in the temple with his big, bulbous head. "Can you give me a clue? What did I do?" She thumbed over her shoulder to the bull pen where the detectives and uniforms worked when they were in the office. "Did those guys in the elevator complain about me or my gruesome twin out there? I swear I didn't let Dougie touch them."

"You didn't do anything wrong." Brooke Kincaid looked up from her computer and smiled. The gesture was meant to reassure her, but that smile shifted into an apologetic frown, leaving Carly feeling anything but. "I'm still not sure what's going on, other than I've pulled service records and promised that anything I see or hear can't leave this office. By the way, are you okay?"

"Nothing that an ibuprofen won't cure. I've been hurt worse wrestling with Frank and Jesse." Although, unlike the man she'd brought in for booking, her older brothers hadn't meant her any real harm. They'd simply been picking on her for getting in their space or being the annoying little sister who'd done her best to keep them fed and dressed in clean clothes after their mother had died. Carly nodded toward the hallway where she'd passed the other two female officers and the geeky-looking guy who'd been flirting with Emily Rangel. "Does it have something to do with them? Am I getting transferred? A reprimand in my file?"

"I don't think it's anything bad." Brooke stood, resting a hand on her pregnant belly as she circled the desk to get close enough to whisper. "The guy in there with Joe is an honest to gosh prince from a little European country called Lukinburg."

"Lukinburg?"

"I looked it up. There's a delegation here from his country negotiating trade agreements. They're even hosting a ball, a fund-raiser for scientific research, while they're here in the US."

"A ball? Like dancing and sparkly gowns? Men in tuxedos?"

"The same."

"What's he doing here at the precinct?"

Brooke crinkled up her nose and sat back on the edge of her desk before answering. "Everything's all hush-hush. The prince called early this morning and asked to see Captain Hendricks as soon as I could fit him into the schedule. You should have seen it when he arrived—he has bodyguards."

"I met them in the elevator. That explains why

they said, 'Save the prince' when Dougie went wacko on me."

"He called me *madam* and he bowed when he introduced himself—Ivan Mostek. He's no Atticus…" Brooke smiled, referring to her husband, the detective who oversaw the task force Carly was assigned to. "But he's hot. He's not soft underneath that suit and those manners. I think he could take care of himself if he had to."

Hearing Brooke refer to anyone besides her husband as hot was something new. Bowing and madaming certainly didn't sound like the visitors they usually got around here, either. Carly's heart rate wasn't slowing down. "He runs his own country? And he wants to see me?"

She glanced down at her dirty clothes and ruined steel-toed boots that she'd borrowed from her older brother Frank, who ran a construction business. It was already ninety degrees at lunchtime, and she'd been out most of the morning working her contacts. Dougie had taken exception to her interfering with his gross habit of flashing and had peed on her. The fact that there had been so much traffic through the old burned-out Morton & Sons Tile Works warehouse near the Missouri River had been reason enough to follow Freeland inside. But when she found him strutting his wares with a young prostitute she was certain was underage, Carly had broken her cover and placed him under arrest. Tackling him in a pile of charred debris from the fire and rolling in dust and ash that had been there for four years had turned her disguise from homeless to filthy.

She held up her hands, admitting the obvious. "I'm hardly looking my best."

"Or smelling it." The phone buzzed on Brooke's desk and she pushed to her feet. "That's Joe. He said there's a time crunch on whatever Prince Ivan needs. You'd better get in there." Brooke's nose crinkled up again and she clapped her fingers over her mouth, looking as if she might be sick. "You're a little ripe."

Carly instinctively retreated a step. "Sorry about that. Dougie didn't come quietly when I arrested him."

"The baby seems to make me really sensitive to smells right now." She turned her head to the side to inhale a deep breath, then reached out to Carly. "Better let me take your coat, at least."

Nodding her thanks, Carly quickly shed her brother Jesse's old duster coat from his cowboy days. That phase had lasted about two months, once he realized that a real working cowboy got a lot dirtier and smelled a lot worse than the ones he'd seen in the movies. Not all that different than what she was smelling like right now. She didn't have to be pregnant to know how Dougie's crude attempt to scare her off had left its mark on her.

She plucked the white T-shirt she wore away from skin that was damp with perspiration and tucked it beneath the belt and holster on her jeans with the holes in the knees. Then she adjusted the chain that held her badge around her neck as if it was a piece of jewelry that could dress up her poor girl from the streets look and gave Brooke a hopeful smile. "I don't look too scary?"

"It'll have to do."

Brooke turned her toward the captain's office just as Joe Hendricks opened the connecting door with an impatient whoosh of air. "Valentine. Good. You're here." He shifted his attention to Brooke while Carly sidled past him into his office. "We're not to be disturbed. Not even if his men call."

"Yes, sir."

The door closed behind her and Carly stopped in her tracks as the man with coal-black hair that she'd seen through the windows rose to greet her. The tailoring of his suit emphasized the width of his shoulders and tapered waist, making him appear taller, though she guessed he was about six feet in height. He practically clicked his heels together and offered her a curt nod. *Bowing.* Wow. Had any man ever been so formal about meeting her before? "Officer Valentine. I am pleased to meet you."

"Hey." Was she supposed to say something more? Shake his hand? No. Not in the shape she was currently in. "Nice to meet you."

The captain gestured to one of the two guest chairs while he circled around to his side of the desk. "Take a seat, Valentine."

With a nod, Carly tore her gaze from their guest and perched on the edge of her chair. Partly because it helped her sit up straight and gave her a stronger posture, and partly because she was painfully self-conscious about her soiled clothes leaving a stain on the beige fabric. "Will this take long, sir? I promised Gina Cutler that I'd cover her citizen self-defense training class after work, so she and Mike can go to birthing class." It seemed that several of her friends were well beyond her in the get-married-and-start-a-family department. "I'd like to grab a shower before then. I think the class would like me to, as well."

Her attempt at humor fell on deaf ears. "This will take as long as it needs to." The captain loosened the tie that cinched his collar and gestured to the man seated beside her. "I'd like to introduce you to His Royal Highness, Prince Ivan Mostek of Lukinburg."

Carly pushed to her feet. "Wait. Should I have curtsied?" She skimmed her hands over the hips of her frayed jeans and frowned at the stains on her boots. "I'm so sorry. I would have changed into my uniform if I'd known I was meeting a dignitary. I just came in off an undercover assignment. I had to blend in with the homeless community in No-Man's Land. I..." She threw her hands up, helpless to deny the truth. "I'm dirty and I stink."

The prince stood when she had risen from her chair. With a perfectly straight face, he said, "All I smell is the smoke from a fire. I trust you were not hurt."

"Aren't you a gentleman?" A nervous laugh snorted through her nose, and embarrassment warmed her face. "Of course, you're a gentleman. You're a prince. I'll be okay. I mean, my pride is shot to..." Carly bit down on that word and the heat in her skin intensified. She was pretty sure that one didn't curse in front of royalty. "I'll have a few bruises, but nothing serious. Thanks for asking." She turned to the captain, silently begging for backup. "Sir, tell me to shut up."

Now the captain chuckled. Great. Way to impress the boss and visiting royalty.

"At ease, Valentine," Hendricks ordered. As he had before, the prince waited for her to sit before he took his seat. She didn't deserve that kind of chivalry with the impression she was making, but his patience with her had a surprisingly calming effect on her nerves, enabling her to concentrate more on what the captain was saying rather than the humiliation she was feeling. "Lukinburg's capital city, St. Feodor, is the sister city of Kansas City. Prince Ivan and his delegation are here for a week to negotiate trade agreements, do a cultural exchange with the Nelson-Atkins Art Museum, meet with local and state officials, host a charity ball at their embassy—you get the idea."

"Uh-huh. What does that have to do with me?"

"The prince has a proposition for you."

Carly turned her attention to the man beside her. Good grief, his eyes were as blue as she'd imagined when she glimpsed them through the office window a few minutes earlier. The lenses in his glasses didn't dim their intensity one bit. Whatever this guy had in mind, it wouldn't be the worst offer she'd ever gotten from a man. Brooke was right, Ivan Mostek was attractive in a polished, faintly arrogant sort of way. In fact, if she met him in a bar, she'd be…lusting after him from afar because she had no clue how to come on to a guy, especially one who looked like he'd stepped out of the self-made CEO section of *Forbes* magazine and was way out of her league. But she'd definitely enjoy her beer and appreciate the scenery from a distance. Still, she knew Captain Hendricks wasn't setting her up on a date. She broke the connection with those penetrating blue eyes and looked to her captain. "What sort of proposition?"

"Captain, if I may?" The prince leaned onto the arm of his chair, close enough to catch a whiff of a scent that was much more pleasant than her own. Something clean, all business, masculine. "Due to instability in my country, as we transfer from a corrupt dictatorship to a democratic society, I am required to step up security. Not every Lukinburger is eager to support the new government."

Ivan articulated every word and avoided contractions. He'd practiced that delivery, so his English would be clearly understood. His tone was less guttural than German, more articulate than Russian, deep in pitch and seductive like fancy poetry. She wondered what that voice sounded like in his native language, whatever language a Lukinburger spoke. Lukinburger? The urge to laugh tickled her thoughts. That made her think of a hamburger. And this guy was nothing but prime steak.

"You find something amusing, Miss Valentine?"

That tone was a little less mesmerizing and a little more *His Imperial Majesty*, and she shook off the inappropriate detour of her thoughts. "Uh, no. No, sir. But I saw your geeky science guy and bodyguards on the elevator. That's not security enough?"

"Geeky science guy?" He repeated the phrase, a question in his eyes. Right. Language barrier.

"You know, nerdy? Thick glasses? Needs a haircut?

I bet if he trimmed that mountain man beard and got the bangs out of his eyes, he'd clean up as good as you."

"I assure you he has showered."

He hadn't understood the slang she'd used. "Clean up as in he'd be attractive if he, you know, took care of himself a little more. Like you." The blue eyes narrowed. Great. She'd just admitted she thought the prince was attractive. Or had she just insulted his friend? "No offense. Clearly, the guy's a charmer. Making a woman laugh is a good thing." Heat crept into her cheeks again. "I'm rambling again. I'm a little self-conscious right now. I don't know the etiquette…am I allowed to have a regular conversation with you?"

"No matter the etiquette, it has not stopped you yet."

Her blush intensified. "Sorry."

"Do not apologize. You are very observant, Officer Valentine. A good soldier should be. I understand that you served in the military before joining the police force?"

"That's right. Army National Guard. That's how I paid my way through school."

"I, too, served in the army of my country. I admire that sense of duty." His compliment altered the heat she felt into a bud of self-confidence. As he went on, steering the conversation toward work further distracted her from her embarrassment. "The man in the hallway is my friend, Aleksandr Petrovic. He is a trusted adviser to me. He has, as you Americans say, a nose for business."

"You mean a head for business? It's a nose for news, a head for business," she pointed out. When his eyes narrowed, she pressed her fingers against her lips and apologized, "I'm sorry. I shouldn't interrupt."

"No. I must use your language correctly." His fingers spanned her wrist, pulling her hand away from her mouth. The light touch sent tendrils of warmth skittering beneath her skin before he released her. She was just as sensitive to the calluses on his manicured fingers, and surprising strength of his hand that she'd associate more with a working man like her father and brothers than a fairy-tale prince. But the charm was certainly there as he bowed his head to her again. "Thank you for the correction."

"You're welcome. You were saying?" Man, was she blowing it in the public relations department. "Your Highness?"

"Ivan will do fine when we are in private like this."

She was supposed to call a prince by his first name? In what universe? Had she taken a harder hit to the head from Dougie than she realized?

"Just as with our embassies in Washington and now Kansas City, we are coordinating with the Department of State and local law enforcement to ensure that our visit here is a safe one—both for ourselves and for your people. Your captain is indulging a personal request while my chief of royal security and his team are meeting with others in your department."

"That makes sense." Carly turned to Captain Hendricks again. "Are you looking for volunteers to work extra duty shifts?"

"Not exactly."

"Then what? Why the private meeting?"

Prince Ivan touched the arm of her chair to recapture her attention. "I need a personal bodyguard. An American who can assist with my understanding of local idioms, someone who knows the city and can provide security specifically for me while I am here."

"You mean a liaison officer between your men and KCPD?"

The men exchanged a look. This time she bit down on the urge to keep talking and waited for one of them to explain why she was here.

Captain Hendricks steepled his fingers together on top of his desk. "The prince believes there is someone inside his delegation who is feeding intel to the dissidents who tried to kill him in Lukinburg. He doesn't know who it is. He's not sure who he can trust."

Carly nodded as understanding dawned. "You're looking for an outsider. Someone who isn't a part of your inner circle." The captain and the prince were looking for a cop who could convincingly portray a member of his security team. Maybe a reporter covering his visit. Or even waitstaff or a maid at their hotel. "You want me to sniff around, see if I can find out anything. I can probably get in and out of your functions without drawing any attention to myself. I'm pretty good at blending in."

"You misunderstand. I want you to be my escort at those functions."

Carly realized her jaw was hanging open, and quickly snapped it shut. "What?"

"His girlfriend," the captain clarified. "He's looking for a female police officer who can be his date at public events. The cover story is that he has an old friend who works at KCPD, someone he met during a military training exercise, and a romance blossomed. His trip to the States has reunited you. She'll provide a level of security no one will question. Someone who can be seen with him, or even stay the night in his hotel room without anyone questioning why you're there."

"Undercover girlfriend? Stay the night?" She snorted a laugh when she heard what the captain was proposing. Then she saw the look in his dark eyes and stopped abruptly. "You're serious? No. No, sir. Do you see what I'm wearing? Do you see how I look?" She pointed to the bull pen. "I'm in the middle of another case. Emily or Detective Wardyn or any other number of female officers would be a better candidate for that kind of assignment than I would."

"Valentine—there were two attempts on the prince's life in Lukinburg."

"The last one was three months ago," the prince added. "I have fresh scars from that explosion. Seven people, including a member of the Royal Guard and the bomber himself were killed that day. I felt that coming to Kansas City would ensure the safety of my delegation, and of your people. By distancing myself from the threat."

Scars? Seven dead? Her panic ebbed at the sobering news. "They tried to kill you?"

"Twice. The bullet missed. The bomb did not."

"And the threat followed you here to the US."

"I believe so." He pulled a note from his pocket and handed it to her.

"You dusted this for prints?"

"There are none," Ivan answered. "At least, not according to my chief of security, Filip Milevski."

"One of the guys you're not sure you can trust?"

"It appeared in my attaché case on the plane during the flight. I do not recall seeing it there when I left St. Feodor."

With a nod from both the prince and Captain Hendricks, Carly unfolded the typewritten note.

Prince Ivan. The false prince.

We won't let you sell our country to the Americans.

We will stop you. Dead.

Lukin Loyalists will rule.

Carly let out a low whistle. "Does Homeland Security know about this? The terrorists may be yours, but they're on our soil." She folded the note and handed it back to the prince. "No offense, pal, but you need to go home."

"Valentine—" the captain chided.

The prince waved off his defense and leaned toward her again. "It is all right, Joe. I appreciate her frankness. Miss Valentine—I cannot tell you for certain that the threats are politically motivated. Perhaps they come from criminals seeking revenge for what the new government has taken from them. It could even be something personal I do not yet understand."

"Personal?"

"Perhaps. This is why I need your help. Whoever is behind this will try again. I want to stop him before any of your people get hurt."

"Prevent collateral damage."

"These trade negotiations must happen to ensure the economic success of my country. I need a strong Kansas City police officer, one who knows undercover work. I need a woman to fulfill this role, one who can handle herself as I saw you handle that criminal out there. I need someone I can trust, who is not influenced by the crown, someone who is there to watch *me* and help *me*. Lukinburg's security contingent are trained Special Forces soldiers. If one of them is against me…" He sat back, lifting his shoulders in a weary sigh. "I would like to have an ally in my corner. I would like it to be you."

She paused a moment to consider what these men were asking of her. "I won't fit in with royalty. I'm working class right down to my dad's plumber's truck. I don't even own a dress."

"We'll get you the right clothes, the right hairstyle, to play the role we need you to. You'd be working straight through the week he's here in Missouri. We'll comp you the time, give you a vacation once the assignment is done."

Prince Ivan nodded. "I will pay for all of these expenses. You will keep anything I purchase for you as a thank-you gift."

"Dressing me up won't make me a lady."

Hendricks rolled his chair back, looking as if this meeting was over and the decision had been made. "You'd be protecting Kansas City by preventing anything from happening to him. You can do this."

"Are you ordering me to?"

"Do I need to make it an order?"

"No, sir. I took an oath to serve and protect my city. That includes its visitors." She stood when the captain did. She was okay with the cop part, investigating and protecting, and with keeping a secret. But the rest of this assignment? She only hoped these men understood what kind of magic it would take to turn her into a woman who would date a prince. "When do I start?"

His Royal Blue Eyes rose and buttoned his jacket. "I need you to start the job now. Right here. Before my people return to the captain's office. I worked as military police when I was in the army, so it is plausible that we are acquainted."

"How long ago did we allegedly meet?" She'd better start prepping for this part if she was to have any chance of pulling it off.

"Two? Three years ago?"

Carly nodded. "I was deployed to Bosnia two years ago. Guarded the base near Tuzla."

"I took part in a training exercise in Sarajevo."

She recognized the city southwest of the base where she'd been stationed. "Then it's believable that we could have met. If the dates coincide."

Captain Hendricks circled his desk. "I'll prep your cover file to make sure they do, in case anyone runs a background check."

Carly inhaled a deep breath. "Then I guess we're doing this."

The prince crossed to the door leading into Brooke's office. "My first public appearance is tomorrow. I am in meetings throughout the day, but I will have lunch with you to go over the information I have on these threats in more detail, and to discuss the protocols my countrymen would expect from a woman I am with. That will give you until tomorrow morning to get whatever you need to look the part. Aleks will set up an account you may use to buy anything you need."

At least she didn't snort this time when she laughed. "I'm gonna need more than a day to make that kind of transformation."

"Make it work, Valentine." Captain Hendricks was done with any more excuses. "You'll be reporting directly to me."

"I hope you don't live to regret this, sir."

"I hope I don't, either."

When she opened the door, Brooke was pouring coffee for the armed men from the elevator. A glimpse of a wire curling beneath their collars reminded her that this was Ivan's security contingent.

"Your Highness." The man with slicked-back dark hair striped by silver sideburns stepped forward. "Coordination with the local police, providing traffic clearance and venue security is in place. They have your schedule and have assured me they have the manpower to provide the backup my team and embassy security will need. I will coordinate the joint agency security team, of course."

"Of course." Ivan laced his fingers through hers, and Carly startled at the unexpected touch. He pulled her up beside him, ashes, grime, stink and all. He hadn't been kidding. The charade was starting right now. "I want to introduce you to my good friend. Miss Carly Valentine. My valued chief of security, Filip Milevski."

Um, uh… *Think, Carly!* Not homeless, not hooker, not task force cop. *Girlfriend.* She summoned a smile. "Hi."

Brilliant. Convincing. Not.

The security chief's dark eyes bored through her with a different sort of intensity than the electricity that charged Ivan's blue eyes. Yep. That was less of a *nice to meet you* and more of a *what the hell?* expression on his clean-shaven face. "This is the woman from the elevator. Why did you not acknowledge her at that time if she is your friend?"

"She was working," Ivan explained, spewing out lies as if they were second nature to him. "Besides, it has been so long since I last saw her—her hair is much longer now and we are both older—I was not sure it was her."

Carly could play the lying game, too. "And I wasn't—I'm not—exactly looking my best. I was a little embarrassed for him to see me like this."

"Nonsense, *дорогой*. You know I love to see a woman in action." What did he say? Huh? Was she going to have to learn a new language for this assignment? Learning to be a proper lady would be hard enough.

Filip Milevski didn't bother to mask his disapproval of her—although whether it was the idea of his boss having a girlfriend or her, in particular, he disliked—and he acknowledged her with a nod and dismissed her at the same time. "I contacted Eduard. Our car is waiting for us out front to take us to the embassy to meet Ambassador Poveda. The rest of the delegation has gone on to the hotel. Galina is discussing protocol with the hotel staff. She will meet us at the embassy."

Ivan's grip tightened around hers, and she got the idea that Milevski's reaction hadn't pleased him. "I will finish introductions first, as you will be seeing more of Miss Valentine throughout the week." He gestured to the sour-faced man with the reddish-brown buzz cut and blotchy skin. "Danya Pavluk. He has worked palace security for years. The Eduard whom Filip mentioned is Eduard Nagy, another bodyguard, specifically, my driver. You will meet him later."

"I look forward to it."

Danya Pavluk looked like making polite conversation pained him. All he said was, "Madam."

"How do you do?"

Danya drank his coffee. Apparently, that conversation was over.

Ivan squeezed her hand again, and she was reminded of the strength and heat of even that casual, deceptively possessive touch. He called to his friend in the hallway. "Aleks, are you ready to leave?"

The nerdy numbers guy said his goodbye to Officer Rangel and came to the doorway. Without waiting for an introduction, he crossed the room to take Carly's free hand. He kissed her knuckles before stepping back and straightening his glasses on the bridge of his nose. "I am Aleksandr Petrovic. It is my pleasure to meet you."

She couldn't help but smile at the way his natural geekiness softened his effusive charm. "Carly Valentine." He looked like a shaggier, softer version of

Ivan. His nose was straighter, his shoulders slightly less imposing. And so far, he seemed to be the friendliest Lukinburger she'd met. "The pleasure is mine."

So these were some of the suspects Ivan thought might betray him to the Lukin Loyalists who wanted to kill him. She'd need to run background checks and spend some time observing and conversing with all the delegation members to get a better read on who was trustworthy and who hated the prince enough to send a death threat.

She made a mental note to make sure she carried a gun or Taser with her at all times. The security men were armed. Pavluk was built like a tank, and though Milevski was older and had more paunch, she suspected he would be equally hard to take down if she had to protect the prince from one of them. And geek didn't necessarily mean defenseless, so she couldn't count Aleks out as a threat, either.

But investigating would have to wait. Sizing up her odds in a physical altercation slipped to the back of her mind, too, when Ivan moved to stand in front of her. With his back to the others, his blue eyes locked on to hers, sending a silent message of gratitude for her alone. Or no, that was a warning. Warning her about what?

Her eyes widened as he dipped his face toward hers and kissed her. Not some fake air-kiss or polite European cheek-to-cheek greeting, either. His firm mouth pressed against the seam of her lips, warmed the spot with moist heat, lingered. His beard and mustache tickled, and she was curious enough about the texture of the dark spiky silk teasing the skin around her mouth that she lifted her free hand to stroke her fingertips across his jaw. The lines of his face were strong, un-yielding. She discovered the firm ridge of a scar hidden near his ear when she stroked against the grain of his beard. From his time in the army? A previous attempt on his life?

A blush of feminine interest in his controlled, masculine touch heated her skin as much as self-conscious embarrassment had warmed it earlier. Every instinct inside her wanted to push her mouth more fully against his. She wanted to part her lips and feel that ticklish heat on the tender skin inside. The kiss was easily the most potent she'd ever received, certainly the most unexpected. Ivan's touch was mesmerizing, magical… *Fake, Valentine! The kiss is fake.*

A pair of invisible fingers snapped beside her ear, waking her from the momentary spell she'd been under. She quickly curled her inquisitive fingers into the palm of her hand and stepped back. She needed a shower and some nice clothes and a seriously intense lesson in royal etiquette before anyone would believe the prince's interest in her was real.

"I will see you tomorrow," he promised.

"Right. Oh." Before he turned, she pulled a card from the wallet behind her badge and tucked it into his jacket pocket. "That has all my numbers on it. If you need to call."

He laid his hand over his heart as if she'd given him a treasure. He looked to Brooke, who stood with one hand curved around her belly, the other clutching the back of her chair, as if she was too shocked by what she'd just seen to stand on her own. Ivan bowed his head. "Mrs. Kincaid. Thank you for your hospitality—and your discretion."

Brooke cleared her throat before she spoke. "Of course, sir. My pleasure."

"Captain Hendricks," he acknowledged. Then Ivan bowed to Carly. "I look forward to our next meeting, *дорогой*."

There it was again. The foreign word rhymed with *the frog boy*. Only it sounded secretive, sensual, anything but insulting, in his deep, accented voice. She wished she had anything half as clever to say. "Me, too."

Ivan and his entourage left, closing the door behind them and heading past a dozen curious glances from the main room to the elevators before Carly released the breath she'd been holding and turned to Brooke. "*Dorogoy*. What's that?"

Brooke typed the word into her computer and pulled up a translation program. "Darling. Sweetheart. It's an endearment."

An endearment. She should have guessed as much simply from the tone of his voice. Oh, he was good at this. Carly seriously needed to step up her game if they had any chance of making this undercover mission work. She also had to remember that the charm and kisses would be fake. She was no fairy-tale princess, and he wasn't really her prince. But he was just shy enough of handsome to make him really interesting to look at. He treated her like a lady, even when she reeked of the streets. And he needed her. It was a potent combination guaranteed to turn her head.

Right then and there she sent her heart a warning that she couldn't have real feelings for Prince Ivan Mostek of Lukinburg. This was a job.

Joe Hendricks's gruff voice sent the same message. "Valentine, you're done for the day. Process your perp and get out of here. Brooke? We need to arrange a leave of absence for Carly. Dismiss Rangel and Wardyn and meet me in my office."

"Yes, sir."

He went back into his office and Brooke grabbed a notepad and pen from her desk. She handed Carly her coat and stood there, searching for the right thing to say. "You're going to explain this to me?"

Of course, she was. Just as soon as she figured out what to say. "Ivan and I go way back. To my army days. I didn't put it all together when you said Lukinburg earlier. I had no idea he was in town. In the country, even." Rambling was never a convincing way to establish a solid cover story. She was supposed to be a better liar than this. "Meeting him…again…was definitely a surprise."

Brooke nodded, still looking confused. "For all of us."

She hated lying to her friend. Not that she didn't trust Brooke completely. But orders were orders. The truth couldn't leave Hendricks's office. Still, she needed a friend who had some relationship experience right about now. "Do you have a place you go to get manis and pedis?"

"Sure. I can get you the number."

"And where exactly does one purchase a ball gown?"

Brooke frowned as if she'd spoken gibberish. "Why?"

"Apparently, for the next week… I'm dating a prince."

Chapter Three

Carly folded her cotton socks down over the tops of the worn leather boots she'd just tied off. She was happy to be in shoes that fit again, happy to be in a tank top and cutoffs instead of a coat that was way too hot for August, happy to be showered and clean and back in the comfort of the home she shared with her father.

Her room, bathroom and the laundry room were down in the basement, while her dad lived on the second floor where her two older brothers had stayed before leaving home to get their own places. Carly didn't mind the low ceilings and cold concrete beneath the carpeted floor. She had enough windows to bring in the summer sunlight, and walls thick enough to give her privacy and quiet from when her brothers and their friends stopped by for a visit. Plus, the freedom to decorate everything down here as she wanted—from the antique oak furniture to the turquoise paint on the walls to the bookshelves crammed with cookbooks, travelogues, romances and fantasy novels that had entertained her for countless hours and were too dear to part with—allowed her to create her own haven from the dangers and stress of her job and the loneliness of her misfit life.

She crossed to the oval mirror above the dresser and pulled a comb through her hair, plaiting the damp waves into a loose braid and securing it with a band. She dabbed some lip balm on her mouth and hurried up the stairs, anxious to get to the kitchen to start dinner before her dad discovered the cherry pie she'd put in the oven. Carly and her father, whom she'd been named after, shared a love of sports, books and sweet things. But while Carly included regular exercise in her daily routine to counteract those sugar indulgences, Carl Valentine was more of an armchair athlete as the back issues he'd struggled with since a work accident some time ago affected him more and more with each passing year. If he got to the pie first, he'd fill up on that and skip dinner. It was a nice compliment to her baking abilities, but hardly the healthy diet she wanted for a man who needed to watch his weight.

Besides, she deserved a piece of that pie and a scoop of ice cream herself after a very long, very weird, very unsettling day.

"Dad? Did you get the grill started?" She hurried through the living room into the kitchen, stopping to pull a pair of hot mitts from a drawer as the timer went off on the oven. "Dad?"

She heard a high-pitched whir of machinery coming from the backyard and paused, cradling the hot plate in her hands. Was that a power saw? That meant company. The odds of getting a slice of cherry pie after dinner just diminished.

The back door leading onto the deck smacked shut as she set the pie on the cooling rack. "Hey, Carly Barley."

With a mock groan, she tilted her face to the muscular man with the wheat-colored crew cut. Her big brother. "Frank. What are you doing here?"

"I had some free time. Thought I'd come over and make those repairs on the deck that Dad's been whining about all summer. He's out back watching the charcoal, making sure we don't burn down the house."

Carly eyed the sawdust sprinkled across his forearms, sticking to the perspiration there. When he reached for the piping hot dish, she nudged him back onto the rug in front of the door, ordering him to brush himself off and wash his hands before he touched any of her food. "Invited yourself to dinner, did you?" She opened the refrigerator to pull out a five-pound package of thawed hamburger and an armload of veggies and condiments.

"Invited myself to find out what's going on with you." When she set everything on the counter beside the stove, Frank was leaning his hip against the lower cabinets, drying his hands. He tucked the towel around the handle of the oven door before crossing his thick arms in front of the Valentine Construction T-shirt he wore. "Are you still available to play on our coed softball team this Saturday? We need you at second base."

Was she free this weekend? She hadn't been informed of Prince Ivan's schedule yet. Was she supposed to forgo her normal life, as well as her regular work hours, to be available for his protection detail

24/7? She was guessing a community league softball game wasn't on his itinerary. She opened the pantry to pull out the spices she needed. "I don't know. I'll have to get back to you."

"I knew it. There *is* a guy." Frank pounded his fist on the counter. "Damn it, I just lost a bet."

"What are you talking about? What bet?"

"Jesse texted that some fancy dude came by the precinct offices to see you." Jesse would be her other big brother, a jack-of-all-trades with an ear for secrets and a mouth that often got him into trouble. His current job as a bartender at the Shamrock Bar, an establishment frequented by several of her colleagues, put him in the perfect place to fine-tune those gossiping skills. "Some officers were in the bar after their shift, talking about this guy. They say he kissed you in front of everybody. I bet ten bucks Jesse was makin' up a story."

"You bet against me?" Embarrassed that her own brother didn't believe in her feminine appeal, she channeled her frustrated anger into the onion she was chopping. "You don't think a 'fancy dude' would want to kiss me?"

"I didn't think any guy would…" He seemed to suddenly realize that the woman glaring at him held a sharp knife in her hand. He wisely backed off a step. "You know how Jesse's always… I mean, the fact that some guy is hittin' on you at all…" His cheeks flushed brick red above the golden scruff on his square jaw. "Jesse also said you were cooking dinner tonight. That you called him to bring beer for the sauce. I've never eaten anyone's food better than yours. That's why I'm here. To eat."

"Pretty weak save, Frank." She split the onion between a saucepan and a sheet tray before pushing him aside to wash her hands. "Now tell me again why you can't keep a girlfriend?"

"I'm sorry." He followed her to the bag of potatoes and back to her cutting board, still trying to make amends for his jab at her ego. She came by her questionable social skills honestly. Although, whether a lack of tact was imprinted in the Valentine DNA, or a by-product of being raised in a motherless household, it was a mystery for the ages. "Do you need me to check this guy out? He's not messin' with you, is he? Those cops said they could tell he had money. He had guys opening doors for him. Drove off in a limo. Guys like that think they can throw around some cash, and girls will—"

"Stop before you stick that big foot of yours any farther into your mouth." Carly didn't consider herself a diminutive woman, but next to Frank, she was downright delicate. That had never stopped her from standing up to him, though. "One, I am a woman, not a girl. I can kiss whoever I damn well please. And two, why is it so far-fetched that a man might like me?"

Despite the square jaw and workingman's build, Frank could still pull off that sweet little boy expression that had gotten her to do more than her fair share of chores growing up and made her forgive him just about anything. "I love you, sis."

Carly shooed him out the back door. "Get out of

my kitchen. Make sure there are no power tools on the picnic table and the deck doesn't collapse by the time dinner is ready. And try to have a little more faith in me, okay?"

Then maybe she'd have a little more faith in herself that she could pull off this assignment.

IVAN STEPPED OUT of the limousine onto the sidewalk. He buttoned his jacket and straightened his tie before sliding his hand into the pocket of his slacks, burning his fingers against the latest gift that had been left for him in his hotel suite. Unlike the flowers, gift baskets and bottles of wine, this one had no color, no wrapping, no welcoming message. It had no words at all on it. Just a set of numbers scrawled across an old black-and-white photograph.

Another death threat.

Carly needed to see it. Someone he trusted needed to know the danger he was facing—the danger a lot of innocent people might be facing if he couldn't unmask who was behind this terror campaign. Who wanted the Prince of Lukinburg dead?

A startled gasp tore him from his thoughts. He took a deep breath that expanded his chest. He nodded to an elderly woman with hair that was as curly and white as the small dog she held by its leash. "Madam."

With her eyes wide and the poodle dancing back and forth across the sidewalk, she eyed him and the black car behind him. "Are you a movie star?" With a squeak of excitement that made the dog yip at her feet, she pressed her hand to her chest. "Did Carl win one of those lottery giveaways?"

He arched an eyebrow at the question he did not understand and smiled. "I am here for Miss Valentine."

Other car doors opened and shut as advisers and security gathered around him. "For Carly? All of you?" The woman scooped the dog up into her arms and stepped closer, dropping her voice to a whisper. "Is this one of those television shows where you pull a prank on somebody? Am I on TV?"

"Why? Have you seen any cameras?" Aleks teased, climbing out of the limousine behind him. Like Ivan, his gaze swept the neighboring houses. Just a normal evening in American suburbia, it seemed. But while Ivan's gaze continued to study their surroundings, Aleks straightened his tie and grinned at the older woman. "How do I look?"

Ivan allowed them their laughter before he made proper introductions. "I am Prince Ivan of Lukinburg."

Her eyes widened with recognition. "I saw you on the news, getting off your plane at KCI."

"We are visiting your beautiful city." He extended his hand. "And you are…?"

"Gretchen Pischnotte. You're really a prince?" He nodded. "What are you doing in this part of town? I've known the Valentines for years. Carl moved in with Carly and the boys right after their mama died."

Carly's mother was deceased? Yet another unfortunate detail they had in common.

Schooling his curiosity to ask for more information about the woman who would be his secret weapon against the traitors who wanted him dead, Ivan fixed a smile on his face. He lightly clasped the older woman's fingers as she gave him a little curtsy. But before she released him, her dog nuzzled against Ivan's hand and licked him. His smile turned genuine. When was the last time he'd been able to run with a dog, or simply pet one? He scratched his fingers over the dog's head. "Who is this little guy?"

A shadow loomed up beside him. "Madam, I need you to move away from the vehicles. Now." Filip Milevski's stern tone made Ivan's stilted conversation sound suave and charming, by comparison. With Filip's right arm blocking Ivan across the chest, pushing him back toward the car, the chief of security pointed up the street. His jacket gaped open, revealing the gun holstered beneath his left arm.

The older woman's skin blanched. "Did I do something wrong?"

"No—"

Filip inched his bulk in front of Ivan. "He is not signing autographs or taking pictures this evening. Move along."

"It was nice to meet you, Mrs. Pischnotte." Ivan bristled at the curt dismissal. With a fearful glance up at Filip, the woman dropped her dog to the ground, and they hurried along the sidewalk that circled the end of the street. She stopped to chat with a man wearing some sort of workman's uniform. He was digging holes in his front lawn. Perhaps not his lawn, since there was a white van in the driveway with a company logo on the side panel. But he seemed to know

Mrs. Pischnotte. With a tired sigh he leaned against his shovel as she took his arm in a fearful grasp, pointing at them in an animated conversation. Ivan pushed Filip's arm away, his glare conveying his displeasure at the needless bullying. "Was that necessary? The idea of this visit is to build a good rapport with our sister city, not show them we are a bunch of thugs like the previous regime. I hardly think an elderly woman is a threat to the throne."

"Is it necessary to be here at all, Your Highness? What about the man she's talking to now? The family next door? I haven't vetted any of these people to see if they're on any kind of watch list. We do not know if the Loyalists' threats have followed us from home." The photograph burned a hole in Ivan's pocket. Perhaps he'd been wrong to keep his security team out of the loop. But a member of that team was as good a suspect as any other passenger who'd been on the plane with him. At least the note confirmed his suspicion that there was a traitor among the royal delegation, someone feeding inside information to the dissidents. No one else would have access to his briefcase. No one else could have taped the photo on the mirror in his penthouse bathroom. "You are not the first leader I have served. I am responsible for your protection. Deviating from your schedule and leaving the hotel to visit your mistress on a whim—"

"You will not refer to Miss Valentine as my mistress, and certainly not in that condescending tone." He waited for Filip to lower his gaze and bow his head slightly. The big man needed the reminder of the hierarchy and just who worked for whom. The fact that Ivan didn't know exactly how this relationship between him and Carly was going to work made him hesitate. All he knew was that she was doing him a favor, and he would not tolerate the snide subtext in Milevski's words. "She is to be treated as an honored guest to the throne."

"As you wish, sir." Filip snapped his fingers for the other bodyguards to split up to do a reconnaissance of the tree-lined street. He made a show of buttoning his jacket, his shoulders bristling with irritation at not being in control of the situation or location. "This is an uncharted part of the city. There are no police officers patrolling the area."

"There is a police officer inside that house." Ivan pointed to the white columns and soft yellow siding on the porch in front of the Valentine home before gesturing to the other houses. "It is a fine neighborhood. The homes and yards are well taken care of." He nodded to the couple in the driveway next door, who'd paused in the middle of loading two boys and bags of baseball equipment into the back of their minivan to watch the interchange between the delegation and their neighbor. "It is hardly the mean streets of the inner city."

"Springing surprises like this on me makes it difficult to plan safe travel routes and make sure my men have time to scout ahead for potential security breaches." Filip waved his hand toward the curve of houses at the top of the street. "This is a dead end. Hardly a street I would have chosen in case we have to make a quick getaway."

It was no surprise that Aleks made a joke to diffuse the tension in the air. "Yes, because that killer poodle was an assassin in disguise. It's a veritable hotbed of terrorist activity here on—" he craned his neck to read the road sign at the corner "—Maple Street."

"Aleks…" Ivan chided, even as he welcomed the levity. Filip didn't share his friend's sense of humor. He wondered if he'd heard Milevski laugh even once since being put in charge of the royal security detail. Still, a growly chief of security with an obsessive need to control Ivan's every movement meant negotiating time alone with Carly would be practically impossible. He desperately needed the normalcy of an informal conversation with someone he knew didn't want him dead just as much as he needed private time to discuss suspects and expand the cover story between them so that no one in the prince's inner circle would suspect the ruse. He smoothed things over with Filip as best he could without surrendering the opportunity at hand. "I will endeavor to give you more warning in the future. But understand that I wish to see Miss Valentine as frequently as possible while I am here in the United States. We have a lot of catching up to do. And my schedule, as you well know, is incredibly busy. Since I have this evening free, I thought it would be fun to surprise her at home."

"Fun?" the security chief growled.

"Honestly, Filip." A woman's cultured, melodic voice chided the man as Galina Honchar stepped out of the opposite side of the limo. The scent of her expensive perfume reached Ivan a few seconds before she did. "Has it been so long since you've been with a woman that you've forgotten all the juicy bits about being in love?"

Filip glared daggers at the raven-haired beauty, but Galina deflected the silent accusation as though flicking away a raindrop. Filip stepped aside as she approached, avoiding a verbal sparring match he had no hope of winning.

She reported on the phone call she'd been finishing up in the car. "I cleared two hours on your schedule for lunch and sightseeing Wednesday, Your Highness. But you will need to be ready for cocktails with the Mayweathers at five thirty. They'll be cohosting the fundraiser ball at the embassy on Saturday. I've noted which suits are to be worn at each event on your phone."

Still in mourning over the death of her fiancé, Konrad, black was her color of choice. Galina had lost a little weight since that fateful day in St. Feodor. But something about losing the man she loved in that bombing had galvanized her into becoming more than Ivan's administrative chief of staff. She would not allow for Konrad's death to be without meaning. Now, Galina guarded the prince's interests as well as his time, serving as an extension of his royal hand. She'd become his emotional protector as well as his personal planner, as they neared his coronation at the first of the new year. She had been efficient before, but now Ivan suspected she could run the palace and even Parliament without him.

Her black suit remained wrinkle-free, despite the long hours of traveling they'd been through today.

"Filip does make a point. Why haven't we heard of Miss Valentine before now? An 'old friend' from your army days?" Galina, a mix of efficiency and deportment, would have made an ideal consort for a prince.

Yet despite her classic beauty and flair for social networking, she did absolutely nothing for Ivan. Even if she didn't still wear her late fiancé's engagement ring, she didn't stir his hormones. Didn't stimulate his curiosity to get to know her on a more personal level. Didn't engender trust with the calculating sharpness of her dark brown eyes and knack for getting things done behind the scenes, handling details he never knew about. He wasn't chauvinistic enough to eliminate her as the traitor in his inner circle simply because she was a woman. He watched everything he said or did around her. Galina, perhaps more than anyone else in this delegation, would be able to spot a charade. Whether or not she was the mole leaking information to his enemies, she would be a hard one to fool. Even if she was innocent, her suspicions would most likely put the real traitor on alert about his relationship with Carly.

Ivan had carefully considered the lies he needed to tell. Ones based on a truth would be the easiest to remember. "I do not say much about my military service and the people I worked with or missions I took part in. And I certainly do not discuss my love life. With anyone," he added for emphasis.

A bright grin appeared in the middle of Aleks's curly black beard. "You never thought you were going to see her again, did you? Now you cannot stand to be this close—in the same country, the same city—and be away from her for a moment longer." He flashed that smile at Galina. "It's called passion, darling. Perhaps yours died with poor Konrad."

"Aleks," Ivan scolded. "You take your teasing too far."

"I am fine, Your Highness." Galina arched one perfectly sculpted eyebrow upward at Aleks, silently informing them both that she was perfectly capable of taking care of herself. "I have not forgotten what love is like. Nor have I forgotten the cause that Kon died for. As long as the indulgence of this affair doesn't distract the prince from the goals at hand, I will support it."

Eduard and Danya returned from their reconnaissance of the nearby homes in the cul-de-sac. Eduard Nagy, Ivan's personal driver, the more sedate of the two, peeled off the sunglasses he no longer needed on the shady street. "Everything looks secure. Almost every house has eyes on us, though. I talked to the man digging up that yard, a Bill Furness. He's the caretaker. The retired couple who lives there is away on a mission trip to Central America for several months. He said the only new residents in the neighborhood are the moles destroying his lawn. He hasn't seen anything unusual." He turned his gaze, scanning the entire neighborhood. "I'll need to pull up the city map on my laptop and mark the through streets and potential bottlenecks in this area if we're going to be frequent visitors."

"We will be," Ivan insisted.

Filip grunted his acceptance before firing off another command to his staff. "Run that watch list of names Homeland Security gave us, too. Make sure there are no potential enemies nearby."

Danya seemed irritated that they hadn't found anyone who seemed an obvious threat. "Your lady friend is cooking on a grill in the backyard, and a man is doing construction work there."

"A man?" Ivan asked. Surely, Carly would have mentioned if she had a boyfriend or fiancé who'd throw a wrench into their pretend relationship.

Danya muttered a word of frustration in their native language. "I didn't take names. I was looking for weapons, not checking out your competition."

Ivan wondered at the anticipation quickening his pulse. It was probably just relief that he'd get to share his suspicions with Carly sooner rather than later. "Just do the job you are paid to do, Danya. And do not use language like that in front of Miss Valentine."

"She speaks Lukin?"

"She understands the tone, if not the words."

Aleks rubbed his hands together in a different sort of anticipation. "You said grilling? I have read that Kansas City is famous for this cuisine. We will be staying for dinner, yes?" He climbed back inside the limo to retrieve the basket of fruit and one of the bouquets that had been delivered to Ivan's hotel room to welcome him. "Perhaps we will bargain for a bite to eat?"

Ivan hated the idea of regifting the items, but he hated to show up empty-handed as well as unannounced even more. He patted the chest pocket where Carly's card rested against his heart. He'd considered calling first, to see if they could meet. But he worried she'd make up an excuse to say no. Plus, upsetting the schedule with this impromptu detour might just put the traitor off his or her game long enough for him to pick up on a clue that might reveal their identity.

Appreciating Aleks's ability to defuse a tense situation, Ivan moved up the sloped driveway to the concrete steps. "We can ask."

Filip lengthened his stride to move ahead of Ivan. "Eduard, stay with the vehicles. Find out what you can online. Danya, you're with me. I'll lead the way. I want to do a sweep inside the house, as well."

Ivan jogged up the second tier of steps onto the raised porch. "I remind you, we are knocking on the front door, not invading a neighboring country."

He bit back the same Lukin curse Danya had used as Filip pressed the doorbell before Ivan could reach it. "Indulge me, sir. I don't have my full team with me in the States. That means I must be more vigilant than ever."

And yet someone had managed to get around that vigilance and send him a death threat. Twice.

Ignoring the urge to point out the failure, Ivan smoothed his fingers over the angle of his beard. "Fine." Flanked by Aleks and Galina, with Danya watching the street from the steps behind them, Ivan motioned Filip to stand aside. "I speak first. I do not want you frightening anyone else."

The inner door swung open, revealing a stocky man with a royal blue and white ball cap pushed back past the receding points of his graying blond crew cut. Although the face was older and male, the green eyes were the same as Carly's. "Mr. Valentine?"

The older man looked at the entourage on his front porch and frowned. "Yeah?"

"I am Ivan Mostek of Lukinburg."

"I'm Carl Valentine of Kansas City," he echoed with sarcasm, raising his voice to be heard over the whir of an electric saw from somewhere in the back of the house. "I ain't interested in anything you're sellin'."

"I am not selling anything."

"Then what do you want?"

"To see your daughter."

Carl Valentine laughed.

Chapter Four

Ivan didn't get the joke.

Apparently, Carly hadn't mentioned him to her father. While it was not allowable for her to share the details of her new assignment, she might have at least prepared her family for the new man who would temporarily be a part of her life. "Is she at home?"

"Is this KCPD business?"

The lies came more easily as he grew impatient. "This is a social call."

His thin eyebrows arched toward the brim of his ball cap. The grinding noise of the saw stopped abruptly, leaving the shock of Carl Valentine's incredulous words filling the room. "Like a date?"

Carl's obvious surprise at meeting the man who'd come to call on his daughter was hardly the kind of reaction that lent believability to this relationship. "Sir, Carly and I—"

"Dad, if that's Jesse, tell him I need one of those beers right away." He was relieved to hear Carly's voice shouting from the kitchen. "Then he can be a lazy butt and watch the game."

"You got company, Carls." Her father stepped back from the door and invited Ivan and the others onto the landing that opened into the living room and split into stairs going up and down to his left. "Better get in here, girl."

"What are you talking about?" Carly strolled into the main room, drying her hands on a towel. "I still have to finish the potato salad... Ivan?"

She stopped in her tracks when she saw the prince and his entourage. It took a split second for her startled expression to soften into a smile, and in that moment, he breathed a sigh of relief. Yes, she'd be able to play this undercover role. Even on the fly like this.

But relief wasn't the only thing he was feeling. She had on no makeup, but that only revealed that her skin was tanned and smooth, glowing with a sheen of perspiration. Her hair was a rich mix of caramel and wheat, and it hung in a loose braid over her shoulder. Even the black leather boots with the thick soles and scuffed, gray toes looked sexy on her, their heft balancing the athletic curve of her legs and making them look impossibly long in those raggedy denim shorts. His body hummed with an awareness that was as invigorating as it was foreign, since he'd purposefully shut down any male needs months ago when he'd agreed to take this position. Carly was no conventional beauty. But she was unique. Intriguing. He suddenly wished he knew her as well as he pretended to.

Their gazes locked for several moments before he realized she was struggling with the protocol of the unexpected meeting. "Should I have said, Your Highness?"

He put up a hand, urging her, and reminding himself, to relax. "Ivan will do fine."

When he took a step toward her, her father put out his hand to stop him. "Wait a minute. You're a prince? Like, you're going to be a king one day? In my house? For my girl?"

The moment Carl's hand touched Ivan's shoulder, Filip was there. With a sweep of his hand, he sent Danya up the stairs and poked his finger in the middle of Carl's chest, knocking him back a step. "No touching."

Carl swatted the offending finger away. "What are you doing? Where is he going? This is my house."

"Filip!" Ivan grabbed the security chief himself and dragged him back to his side. "We are guests."

He needn't have bothered. Carly moved in front of her father, her eyes locked on to Filip like a lioness siting her prey. "It's okay, Dad. This is Prince Ivan's security team. They're checking the house. Your man will find my father's hunting rifle locked in a gun cabinet in his bedroom closet. My badge and service weapon are in a lockbox downstairs beside my bed. My brother is out back using power tools. Otherwise, we're unarmed." Although her demeanor remained calm, there was no mistaking the warning in her tone. "If you ever touch my father like that again, I will break that finger."

Ivan swallowed a grin as she faced off against the man who was twice her size. Either deciding a confrontation wasn't good for international relations, or perhaps wondering if she could make good on that threat, Filip offered the Valentines a curt nod and hurried down the stairs. "My apologies."

After tucking the towel into the back pocket of her shorts, she tilted her eyes up to Ivan, sending a silent look that was filled with frantic questions. *Why are you here? Did something happen?*

When we're alone, he wanted to answer.

Her words came out in a surprisingly casual tone. "I thought we were meeting tomorrow. For lunch."

"I could not wait that long to see you again. Is it rude if I invite myself to dinner?" He sniffed the sweet, spicy smells coming from the kitchen and wafting around her. "It smells delicious."

He was as aware of everyone in the room watching them as he was of her transformed appearance. If they were alone, this meeting might go very differently. But with an audience, he took her hand and played the attentive suitor. He leaned in to press a kiss to her cheek, lingering longer than he intended because he couldn't resist inhaling the essence of something tasty on her warm skin. Although he still detected a faint wisp of smoke clinging to her, her scent was cinnamon-y, with a hint of onion and something warm, like molasses or brown sugar, just like the food he smelled from the kitchen. Carly's homey, natural scent was much more appealing than the stain of body odors that had wafted about her at their meeting earlier in the day. He pulled away, stroking his fingertip across her cheek to remind her to blink instead of looking so stunned by his attention.

Her voice was a breathless whisper, for his ears alone. "Are you going to kiss me every time we meet?"

He answered just as quietly. "Are you going to blush every time I kiss you?"

If anything, the rosy tone on her cheeks intensified and she pulled away. She cleared her throat before addressing him in a normal voice. "I swear I don't always smell like ashes. I've been wrestling with the grill out back." She smiled up at her father. "Somebody left the bag of charcoal out in the rain."

"I said I was sorry." Blushing much like his daughter, Carl quickly changed the conversation. "You might as well stay. Carly's been fussin' over a big dinner. Plenty of food. You folks like baseball?" he asked, gesturing into the living room where the television was broadcasting a sporting event. "The game's about to start."

Ivan gave him an honest answer. "It is not a sport we play often in Lukinburg. I follow football, er, soccer. But I wish to learn more about your country."

Aleks stepped up beside Ivan, hugging the flowers and fruit basket against his chest. "I understand your team is called the Royals? That seems to be a fortuitous sign with the prince here. I would like to watch."

Carl nodded. "They're actually named after the American Royal livestock show that's been around since we had stockyards and cattle drives in KC. But it sounds like good luck to me. Come on in and sit."

"Thank you." Needing no other invitation, Aleks pushed the flowers and basket into Carly's arms and followed her father to the sectional sofa.

Galina took his place at Ivan's side, extending her hand. "We have not had the pleasure to meet. I am Galina Honchar, His Royal Highness's chief of staff. I coordinate his appearances and manage his schedule."

Juggling the gifts she held into one arm, Carly reached out to shake the other woman's hand. "Carly Valentine. Nice to meet you. I…date him."

"Whatever you are cooking smells amazing." Ever an icon for etiquette, Galina asked the question Ivan should have. "Are you sure we are not imposing?"

"It's not fine dining, but you're welcome to stay." The basket and flowers teetered over the edge of Carly's arm, and Ivan reached out to grab the cellophane-wrapped basket of apples and oranges before they hit the floor, forgetting for a moment that the future leader of Lukinburg did not haul anything, especially when there was staff there to do it for him. "Thanks. I'm grilling burgers." She grinned. "For Lukinburgers." As quickly as she'd smiled, she frowned. "Wait. That's not an insult, is it?"

Galina laughed politely as Ivan hastened to reassure Carly. "Not if the food tastes as good as it smells."

Or as good as Carly smelled.

Her smile reappeared, and Ivan suddenly felt as successful as he would once the Kansas City agriculture and trade officials signed the new business contracts with his government.

But any feeling of victory was short-lived when the front door burst open behind him. A young man with shaggy brown hair, wearing a T-shirt and a leather vest entered with a bellow. "What the hell are those cars doing out front? I had to park way... Whoa."

The security team returned in a blur and shoved the young man up against the wall. He lifted the six-pack of bottled beer he carried out of Danya's way when the bodyguard felt beneath his leather vest and patted down the sides of his jeans. "Hey, pal, you ought to buy me dinner first."

"Danya." Ivan ground the order between clenched teeth. "Retreat."

The bodyguard pushed to his feet. "He is not armed."

Green eyes. Square jaw. Another Valentine. Great. He was scoring zero points in the public relations department with this family. But the young man didn't seem to mind the rude greeting once his gaze landed on Galina. Instead of complaining about the welcome, he smiled. "Nice. Wish you'd have frisked me."

"Jesse!" Carly chided. Including the young man and Danya in her glare, she slid between the two of them, motioning for Danya to back away. "This is my brother Jesse. If you try to frisk my brother Frank, he'll punch you."

She linked her arm with her brother's in protective solidarity. Her smile tightened into a grim line as she went through the introductions. "His Royal Highness, Prince Ivan. The prince's friend, Aleksandr Petrovic. His chief of staff, Galina Honchar. Chief of security Filip Milevski. And Danya... I'm sorry, I didn't catch your last name."

"Pavluk."

"Have the Russians invaded?" Jesse asked.

Danya stepped forward, taking the joking remark as an insult. "We are not Russian. We are proud citizens of Lukinburg."

"Oh, hell. It's true. Hey, Frankie! You here? You owe me ten bucks." The rhythmic pop of a nail gun that had underscored the entire conversation stopped as the young man extended his hand. "Nice to meet you, Ivan. What's your business with my sister?"

Before he could answer the question, another Valentine entered through the kitchen. This one was bigger, blonder, but the family resemblance was the same. "What are you on about now, Jess?" He pulled a ball cap off his head to mop at the sweat on his brow and pointed the cap at Danya. "You're that guy I saw lurking around the Fitzes' yard. What are you doin' in our house? With guns? The kids don't need to see those."

"It's okay, Frank. My older brother." Carly made the round of introductions again, and Ivan shook his hand. He didn't like admitting the relief he felt to learn this was her brother, and not a potential rival for her time and attention.

Frank Valentine appeared to be about the same age as Ivan, in his early to midthirties. He crossed his brawny arms over his chest. "You really a prince?"

"Are you really her brother?"

Jesse, clearly the more outgoing of the two, laughed. "A wiseass, huh?"

Carly pinched his arm. "You don't say things like that in front of—"

"It is fine." Apparently, plain speaking was a Valentine family trait. Ivan could appreciate that. In fact, he envied their openness. He didn't have to second-guess what they were thinking and if they were plotting against him. "Before I had to bow to royal protocol, I, too, had a penchant for sarcasm. It still slips out every now and then."

"I'll take this off your hands." Galina plucked the fruit basket from Ivan's grip and moved forward to take Frank Valentine's arm. "It is time for us to leave the prince to the reason for his visit. Spending time with Miss Valentine. Filip, Danya—perhaps you should check with Eduard to see what information he has discovered?" After the security team exited onto the porch, Galina's smile included an invitation for Jesse to join her and Frank. Both men seemed eager to oblige. "Teach me about this baseball."

While the others settled in front of the television, Ivan followed Carly into the kitchen. "Does no one help you prepare the meals?"

"I like to cook. This is my therapy when I need to think." After setting the flowers on the counter, Carly stirred beer into the pot bubbling on the stove. Then she opened the refrigerator and took out a tray of hamburger patties. She peeked into the living room, confirming that everyone was busy with the game or engrossed in conversation, then dropped her voice to a whisper and hurried to the back door. "Does that jacket come off?" she asked when he moved in beside her to hold the door open. "You might want to roll up your sleeves and loosen your tie. It's hot out here."

Sensing the urgency in this sudden shift in behavior, Ivan shrugged out of his jacket and draped it over the back of one of the kitchen chairs before following her down the steps into the backyard. He joined her at the grill. "I need to speak with you privately."

"I didn't think you were here for a booty call."

He folded the crisp white cuffs of his sleeves. "I do not understand."

"You know, when a guy calls or drops by to…" Her cheeks blushed bright pink and she shoved the tray into his hands, asking him to hold it while she added the extra burgers to the grill and slipped ones that were already cooked to a warming bin.

"Carly, I need you to speak always so I understand you. What is *booty call*?"

"A quickie. Sex." She patted her backside. "It's slang for this. That guys want to… Women, too…" Her cheeks heated with another blush that he doubted could be attributed to the hot coals or humid summer weather, and she went back to flipping burgers. "That's why your friends think you're here, isn't it? Why you want to see me? Only you and I know the truth."

Ivan's gaze had settled on the curve of her denim shorts the moment she'd touched herself there. What was wrong with him? Why did this earthy woman make him forget every bit of protocol that had been trained into him? Why did he care if she blushed adorably when he paid attention to her or feel a knife-hot urge to defend her when anyone said something demeaning or took advantage of her? But he remembered the photo, he remembered his duty to his country, he remembered the promise he'd made to her police captain, and politely raised his focus to her eyes. "I will remember this slang. Because you have a memorable booty."

"Um… Thank you?" She took the empty tray and set it on the shelf beside the grill. "Tell me why you're here. We weren't supposed to meet until tomorrow, so something must have happened."

Ivan nodded. His shoulder brushed against hers as he turned, keeping his back to the living room windows, in case there were curious eyes on them, and pulled out the mutilated photograph. "I did not know who else to trust with this."

She closed the grill and took the photo from him. "It looks old."

"I am afraid its meaning is new." He pointed to the rectangular image, in shades of gray and black, centered in the picture. "It is the flag of Lukinburg, draped over a coffin. It is an historic picture. The last rightful king was assassinated shortly after the Second World War. A bomb went off at his summer house on Lake Feodor. He lay in state in the palace. A few months later, while the government was in transitional chaos, there was a coup. Our democratic government as we knew it was over."

"Until you stepped in?" Carly tilted worried eyes up to his, keeping her arm flush against his so she could return the photograph without being seen. "It's dated this upcoming Saturday."

"It is the night of the embassy ball." The message might be symbolic, but the meaning was clear. If he didn't step down, *he'd* be the next head of state lying in a coffin. And his death would happen on Saturday.

"It was left in my hotel suite. Anyone in my delegation could have put it there. We held a meeting there this afternoon."

"Someone on the hotel staff, or pretending to be, could have left it."

He shook his head as he folded the photo and stuffed it back into his pocket. "Filip has limited the staff who has access to my suite. He personally ran background checks on each of them and cleared them."

"He could have cleared someone with ties to the Lukin Loyalist movement. You think he's your mole?"

"I do not know." The heat and humidity of the summer evening burned through Ivan's skin, reminding him of the pressure building inside him since he'd agreed to take this job. If he had a clear enemy, he'd know how to handle this. But the mind games, the threats, the collateral damage that could result if he made a mistake—how was he supposed to fight that?

Carly bumped her shoulder against his, drawing him from the dark turn of his thoughts. "The obvious question is—can you cancel the ball?"

"No."

"Right. Too important to you and your country." She glanced behind her, then laced her fingers with his down between them. "How many messages like this have you gotten?"

Was her touch for comfort? Or for show? Was someone watching them? Ivan decided he didn't care. He liked the sure grip of her hand in his as much as he liked everything else about her. He tightened his fingers around hers, absorbing some of that strength.

"Two since I've touched down here in the US. Several more back in Lukinburg. I believe they are trying to scare the prince into abdicating the throne, letting someone more malleable lead the new government."

"The prince?" She laughed softly. "You just referred to yourself in the third person."

"Did I?" Perhaps jet lag was getting the better of him. Or stress. No wonder he couldn't keep his thoughts straight. He needed to be on point every waking moment if he was going to accomplish all he'd set out to do. Who was he kidding? He couldn't even afford to sleep without being on guard for his life.

"It's probably easier to think the threats and attempts on your life are happening to someone else."

"Perhaps." The marks of the injuries peppering his neck and back burned with the enormity of the challenge he faced. "Yet I am the one with the scars. If they cannot frighten me from my duty, then they will kill me."

"No pressure, hmm?" She released his hand to reach up and trace her fingertip against the scar that cut through his beard. Although it was meant to be a comforting gesture, every nerve ending seemed to rush to the spot, pulsing beneath her touch. The moment he thought the contact might mean something more to her, too, she pulled away and went back to work, opening the grill and flipping the hamburgers. The hiss and pop of the moisture hitting the coals masked her words as much as the steam and smoke hid their expressions from any curious onlookers. "All right. I'll talk to Captain Hendricks, and we'll try to get as many people undercover next Saturday to beef up security as we can. We can put SWAT teams on alert and lock the embassy down as tightly as possible without alerting your traitor. You and I will have an emergency evac plan in place that Milevski doesn't know about. In case it's him."

"I will make sure you have an opportunity to tour the embassy this week."

"In the meantime, I'll do everything I can to identify whoever is behind the threats and get him out of the way before Saturday night."

"*We* will do this. We will work together."

"We're a team. The prince and the commoner. The European and the American. The uptown leader of his own country and the downtown nobody." She closed the grill before pulling the towel from her back pocket and wiping her hands. "Are you sure your people are buying this between you and me? A few kisses and holding hands are one thing, but somebody's still going to have to teach me how to dance."

"I would be honored to do this." She thought of herself as a nobody? How could any man miss her vibrant energy and brave spirit? There were beautiful green eyes in that ordinary face. And, judging by the awareness still fizzing through his blood, he was extremely glad that he'd added the word *booty* to his English vocabulary. "It would not be a lie to say I find you attractive. Perhaps you are not the typical royal consort, but that part, I do not have to pretend. Thank you for helping me."

"Nobody's blowing up anyone in Kansas City on my

watch." She tilted a smile up to him. "And nobody's blowing up our most honored guest."

Answering that smile with one of his own, he turned her into his arms. "First lesson." Her forearms flattened against his chest and she was suddenly stiff, as if bracing herself for something unpleasant. He placed her left hand on his shoulder and folded her right fingers into his palm before settling his hand at her waist. "A simple waltz is three steps. Right, left, right. Left, right, left. Your feet move the same direction as mine, like a reflection in a mirror."

One boot came down on the toe of his polished oxford. "Sorry. Clearly, these aren't the right shoes for this."

"Again. Right, left, right. Left, right, left. Feel my hands pull you with me when we turn."

"There's a turn?" She froze. Stomp. Ivan gritted his teeth at the pain stabbing through his little toe. "Sorry."

When she tried to push away, he tightened his hold on her waist. "Carly, do you practice any kind of martial arts or fight training?"

"Of course, I do. It's required to maintain my badge. I run, kickbox, do yoga once a week to take a break from working out."

"This is no different than learning an attack sequence or exercise routine. Memorize the pattern. Then feel your way through it." He shifted her in his arms, pulling her hips against his. "Do you feel the rhythm when I move?" She nodded, still trying to peek over his arm down at the patio. "Look in my eyes, not at our feet. My arms and thighs will lead you in the direction you need to go."

Those pretty green eyes fixed on to his. Ivan hummed a strain from Strauss, emphasizing each downbeat. Gradually, she relaxed against his arm at her waist and she eased the death grip on his shoulder. This time, she spun with him in a dramatic turn. "I'm doing this."

There were only a few more stumbles of her boots knocking against his shoes before he swept her into a turn. She laughed until a snort made her pull up with embarrassment. He pressed a kiss to the bridge of her nose, enjoying the genuine sound of delight before pulling her into step again and waltzing across the patio with her.

She was humming *The Tales of the Vienna Woods* with him when the back door burst open and her brother Jesse ran out onto the deck. "Carly! Get in here. Something's wrong with Frank."

Her smile vanished. The music stopped. The grill was forgotten. She charged up the stairs. "Frank?" Ivan ran into the living room behind her. He paused in the archway, taking in the convulsions of the big man writhing on the floor. "Frank!" Carly dropped to her knees beside her brother, grabbing at his stiff arm. "He's having a seizure. What happened?"

"Is he epileptic?" Ivan asked.

"No."

He spotted the cellophane ripped off the fruit basket. Galina was picking up fruit that had spilled out and rolled across the carpet. Frank crushed the remains of an apple core in his fist. This was familiar somehow. But how did he help?

Carl Valentine was on the phone to 9-1-1. "My son—"

"Tell dispatch I'm with KCPD," Carly shouted, giving her badge number. "Get a bus here now." Carly turned Frank onto his side as her father continued the call. Ivan knelt beside her, helping her position the big man as his back arched and he became harder to control. "Don't let him hit the fireplace."

Jesse knelt opposite her, the three of them fighting to keep Frank in a position where he could still breathe and not knock into any furniture. "He said he couldn't wait until dinner. First, I thought he was choking. I tried to give him the Heimlich. Then he started doing this."

Carly slipped a pillow beneath her brother's head and held it in place. "He's burning up."

Ivan had never witnessed a fit like this himself, but he'd seen pictures, training films when his unit had been briefed on nerve gases and other toxins that had been hidden and forgotten in eroding bunkers and old army bases from World War II. One of his earliest assignments had been with a team sent in to destroy any weapons that could leech into the environment or be accidentally triggered by an innocent explorer who happened upon them.

Aleks tiptoed past him and squeezed his shoulder. "We need to get you out of here. This is not the kind of publicity—"

"No!" Ivan shrugged off his touch. "I know this. It

was a torture from the old days. Strychnine." He pried the smushed apple from Frank's hand and sniffed the bitter chemical smell of the pulp. Galina was reaching for an orange that had rolled over by the brick hearth. "Do not touch that!" The startled woman snatched her hand back. "He has been poisoned. We must get him to a hospital right away."

"Ambulance is on its way," Carl reported, kneeling beside Jesse. "They said he only has a couple of hours before the internal damage becomes irreversible. Son?"

But Frank couldn't respond.

Ivan didn't bother stating the obvious, not when another man's life hung in the balance. Not when Carly could lose her brother.

That fruit had been a gift to him.

He was the one who should be dying.

Chapter Five

Ivan stood the moment the door to Frank Valentine's room opened. Saint Luke's Hospital was quiet, yet surprisingly busy for this time of night. His eyes burned with fatigue after being up for over twenty-four hours, but he didn't intend to sleep until he knew for certain that he hadn't gotten Carly's brother killed, and that there wouldn't be lasting effects from the poison.

So many lives were impacted by every choice he made. But he didn't intend for his desperation, his utter isolation from people he could trust, to ruin the life of the woman he was foolishly learning to care for in a very short time. Carly Valentine felt like salvation to him, like something real despite the charade of their relationship. She was the touch of humanity he'd been missing from the pomp and circumstance of his life as the crown prince.

The doctor came out first, chatting with Joe Hendricks, who'd been called in to take the official report for the police department. Carly followed next, with her father and Jesse right behind her.

Still in her tank top, cutoffs and boots, Carly now

wore her gun holstered on her belt and her badge hanging around her neck. Despite the tough facade, there was something vulnerable about the way she ran her hands up and down her bare arms and hugged herself. There were small divots of shadow beneath her eyes now, indicating fatigue and stress, even as she hung on to every word exchanged between the doctor, the captain and her father.

"Give me a few minutes with Miss Valentine." He paused when Filip shot to his feet, preparing to follow. Ivan put up his hand, warning him that he didn't need any help walking across the room. "Send the others back to the hotel. A few of us, at least, should get some sleep before the meetings tomorrow morning. I plan to stay until I get a full report on Frank Valentine, and I know Carly is all right."

"As you wish. I will also be staying."

Ivan tipped his head to the sterile ceiling, his nostrils flaring with a measured breath. He admired Filip's dedication to his job even as he found his need to hover irritating. Or was his attentiveness something more purposeful? Like keeping his prey in sight? An instinctive male need to call him on his behavior had to be squelched. "You have been up longer than I have. Leave Danya or Eduard and get some rest. I will have Captain Hendricks with me. I am perfectly safe."

Filip adjusted the flak vest he wore beneath his shirt and jacket, as if the protective armor didn't quite fit his muscular bulk. Maybe he didn't feel comfortable wearing it, if his next words were any indication. "I failed to protect you this evening. I should have checked every delivery myself. I will not fail again. I am staying."

Ivan nodded. He wished he could trust this long-time servant to the crown without hesitation. Right now, he could only act as if he did. "Very well. But, privacy? Please?"

Filip gestured to the end of the hallway. "I have secured a room for you, just around the corner. I anticipated you would wish to speak to Miss Valentine. You will not be disturbed. I will dismiss the nonessential personnel and wait for you here."

"Thank you."

With a sharp nod, Filip crossed the waiting area to speak to his team, plus Aleks and Galina and a pair of uniformed officers who had accompanied Captain Hendricks to stand watch and keep a trio of local reporters away from the family and the royal entourage. Ivan shrugged off his suit jacket and went to join Carly the moment the doctor excused himself.

Up close, Ivan could see the goose bumps dotting Carly's skin. He hadn't imagined the chill she felt. He draped his jacket around her and squeezed her shoulders in a subtle show of support before moving in beside her to join the circle of hushed conversation. "Is Frank all right?"

She clutched the jacket together at her neck, offering him a weak smile of thanks. "Dr. McBride said Frank probably feels like he's been hit by a train with the severity of those muscle spasms and pumping his stomach. He's on pain meds. Stimuli might trigger new seizures until it's completely out of his system, so they're keeping him mildly sedated in a quiet, dark room."

"Barring any complications, the doc says he's going to pull through." Carly's father looked as if he'd aged since they'd first met earlier that evening.

Even her smart-mouthed brother seemed subdued by the close call. "I've always looked up to Frank. He's the strong one. Seeing him hooked up to all those IVs and beeping machines freaks me out as much as seeing him writhing on the floor did."

Carly linked her arm through Jesse's and rested her head on his shoulder. "Dr. McBride said everyone's quick actions, including yours, saved him. Frank *is* strong. He's too stubborn to die. Focus on that."

Jesse leaned over to press a kiss to her temple. "Nice pep talk, Carls. But we all know this was no accident. Are you gonna get this guy for us?"

"Of course, she will." Carl winked at his daughter. "That's her job."

Not for the first time, Ivan wondered at the balance in this family. Was Carly a strong woman by nature? Or was she forced to be that way because her brothers and father needed her to take care of them? "Mr. Valentine, I am sorry that your son was hurt, when clearly, I was the target. I wish to pay for any medical expenses—"

"Did you poison Frankie?"

"Of course not."

"I didn't think so. So don't apologize. And don't think you gotta throw your money around to make up for what happened to my boy. You've got enemies, Your Royalness. And if you're going to be dating my daughter, that means we have enemies, too. But you're not one of them. Of course, you hurt my little girl and all that changes."

How was he supposed to respond to that? He would never intentionally hurt Carly. And yet, he feared he already had. "Sir—"

"Dad..." Carly began.

Carl removed his ball cap and waved off both of their protests. He rubbed the top of his head down to his nape, sighing as if that burst of anger had drained whatever stores of energy he had left. He clapped Captain Hendricks on the shoulder. "Joe, you get the bastards who did this."

The police captain nodded. "I will."

The other man's promise seemed good enough for Carl. "I'd better sort through that insurance mess."

There was nothing subtle about Carly widening her eyes at Jesse and pointing toward their father as he walked away. It took a split second for him to catch on before he snapped his fingers. "Wait up, Dad. I'll come with you."

He hurried to catch up to Carl and squeezed a hand around his shoulder, offering his support so that none of them would be alone.

Captain Hendricks waited for Carl and Jesse to move out of earshot before he leaned in. "We need to talk. Your Highness?"

Ivan inclined his head toward the bodyguard pacing the waiting area. "There are ears here." Placing his hand at the small of Carly's back, he led them into the private room around the corner. "I wish to hear anything you have to say."

It was no secret that Carly was a cop and that Joe was her precinct commander, so no one questioned why an officer of his authority was on the scene when a crime like attempted murder occurred in the company of a visiting dignitary. But the real gist of their conversation needed to remain between the three of them.

As soon as the door closed behind him, Joe pulled a notepad from the pocket of his jacket. "Since this is such a high-profile case, I expedited the tox results on that fruit basket through the crime lab. Every apple was injected with strychnine."

"Just the apples?" Carly ran her hands up and down the silk-lined jacket that hung around her, as if Ivan's coat alone wasn't enough to chase away the chill she felt. "Why not the oranges?"

Ivan had the answer to that. "The prince does not like oranges."

Her eyes darted up to his, and a tiny frown mark dimpled her forehead. Great. He'd just referred to himself in the third person again. But when Joe didn't mention the odd phrasing, Carly didn't ask the question stamped on her face. She crossed to the minibar that held a steaming pot of coffee but didn't pour herself a cup. "That would narrow down the possibility of the wrong person eating the poison. If it's common knowledge."

"Most of Lukinburg knows this. There was an embarrassing news report during the last orange harvest about how difficult it is to peel an orange. I did not take the time on camera to eat one presented to me. The reporter suggested I hire someone to peel oranges for me. It became a jab at increasing government spending on what some consider to be frivolous programs." That attempt at humor had given the Loyalists some unnecessary ammunition against the new government.

"Are they?" Carly asked, facing him again. "Frivolous? It could be motive for the threats."

"I do not consider bringing in agricultural consultants to reclaim our overtaxed land and increase crop production to feed my people to be a frivolous expense." Ivan bristled at how the old guard resented change, even if it was to their own benefit. "We spend a fortune importing grain and meat. One of our goals during this visit is to negotiate more equal trade with your farmers, as well as meet potential consultants. In the long run, we will save money by doing this."

Joe tucked his notepad back into his jacket. "Save the political speeches for your official appearances. Right now, I'm looking to narrow down our list of suspects. The forensics report wasn't much help." He included both Ivan and Carly in his dark gaze. "The lab dusted the basket and remaining fruit for fingerprints. Somebody wiped it clean."

Carly pushed away from the counter and paced to the door. "I didn't think to secure it right away. I was worried about Frank."

"Actually, it narrows down our suspect list," Joe said. "By the time the lab got a hold of it, the plastic wrap was completely missing. Whoever did it had to be someone at your house, covering his or her tracks."

Carly stopped in front of Ivan, tilting her face to his. "Could he or she have wiped the prints to protect you from being a suspect? You handled the basket."

"So did you. And Galina and Aleks."

"Dad and Frank, too." She shook her head and continued to pace. "There should be a ton of prints."

The rest of Joe's report wasn't much more enlightening. "The lab also matched that first note you showed me to the printer on your airplane. I think we can safely confirm that this is an inside job."

"But is it one person? Or is that inside man the representative of an entire rebel faction? Could there be others from the Lukin Loyalist movement here in Kansas City?"

"If there are, we'll find them. Hopefully, before they make their move." The captain buttoned his collar and straightened the knot of his tie. "In the meantime, I'll have a lab team go through everything in your suite with a fine-tooth comb to see if there are any other threats there."

"You will have to go through Filip for security clearance."

Grinning, Joe buttoned his jacket and headed for the door. "It's a Kansas City hotel, not embassy property. All I need is to wake up a judge and get a search warrant." He turned his dark eyes to Carly. "Sorry about your brother. You okay, Valentine?"

She nodded. "Yes, sir."

"Good. You're going to need sharp eyes and a clear head. I need you with the prince as much as possible until we figure out who the mole is and what his ultimate plan might be. You're our first line of defense and our main source of intel. I want to get ahead of this guy."

"So do I."

Ivan extended his hand. "Thank you, Joe."

They shook hands. "This may have started out as a courtesy to a visiting dignitary. But now they've threatened my town. They've hurt one of my citizens. It's personal."

After Hendricks left, Carly resumed her pacing from the untouched coffee to the door and back again. "Do you recognize the handwriting on that photograph with Saturday's date?"

Ivan propped his hands at his waist, anchoring the center of the small room as she moved past him. "There is not enough to tell, no."

"And the fruit? Who gave you the fruit?"

"There was no card. I assumed it had come with something else. The welcome gifts were all from local officials, companies I am meeting with, the embassy."

"Someone either snuck them in or doctored them after delivery." Her gaze flickered up to his as she walked by again. "Is there a log of every single person who enters your suite at the hotel?"

"Filip would have that."

"And we don't know if he would tell us the truth. If *any* of your people would tell us the truth." She caught the edges of his jacket and hugged herself more tightly inside it. "Have you at least run a background check on everyone in your entourage? Would any of them have a connection to these Loyalists? A family member? A lover?"

He regretted that he couldn't guarantee the answer to that question, either. "Filip—"

"Filip is in charge of that, too." She exhaled on a stuttering breath, and for a split second, he thought she was crying. But there were no tears, only a white-knuckle grip on his jacket and shoulders that were visibly shaking. "It's so damn cold in this hospital."

He caught her by the arm when she walked past and drew her up against his chest. Ignoring the token protest of her hands bracing between them, he wound his arms around her, rubbing large circles against her back. He wrapped her up, jacket and all, absorbing every shiver, warming her with the heat of his hands and body, standing strong for her when she was ready to crumble. He rested his cheek against her temple, tangling strands of her hair in his beard as he whispered into her ear. "Take a deep breath, *dorogoy*. It is the adrenaline crash after so much stress and worry. You have had a long day and are very tired. You will get through this."

Seconds, maybe minutes, passed before she moved. Then her arms snaked around his waist. He felt the imprint of ten fingers fisting into his shirt and pressing into the skin underneath as she burrowed into him, snugging the crown of her head beneath his chin. Ivan widened his stance, letting her move as close as she wanted to be. Comforting this woman—warming her, calming her—seemed like the most useful thing he'd done in the past few months. Feeling capable again, like he was the right man for this particular job, soothed some of the tension he carried inside. He treasured Carly's faith in him and prayed that her trust wouldn't be misplaced. "I am sorry that your brother—"

"Shh. Dad's right. No apologies. It's ninety degrees outside tonight, and I can't get warm. Just hold me a little longer."

He smiled against her hair, liking that she told him what to do, completely ignoring royal decorum and the fact he was about to lead an entire country into the twenty-first century. She didn't need him for who he was supposed to be—she just needed him. "If you insist."

Ivan held Carly until the shivering stopped and comfort changed into a subtle awareness of her sleek, athletic body relaxing against his. Her small breasts pebbled beneath the nubby friction of his jacket catching between them. The scent of her hair reminded him of the laughter they'd shared beside the grill, dancing on her patio. The clutch of her fingers in the back of his shirt eased their grip and flattened against his spine, mimicking the stroke of his hands on her.

A warm sensation pooled around his heart that had nothing to do with the exchange of body heat. He was falling for this woman. He wished he could simply be a man and not a prince, that, like at this moment, her needs were more important than his responsibilities. They were both creatures of duty, both accustomed to hiding any weakness, both isolated by the need to keep their true mission a secret. She had beautiful green eyes, those crazy, sexy legs and a penchant for speaking her mind that made him want to discuss all kinds of topics with her, from politics to what she liked to cook best to how she'd react if he kissed her. A real kiss. Not for show, not for anybody but the two of them. Would she blush again? Would she take charge, or would he have the pleasure of training her how to do that, too?

Carly took a deep breath and pushed away from him, cutting off his errant thoughts. "Where does strychnine come from? Who'd have access to it?"

It took a second for him to switch topics with her. The woman wanted to work.

Ivan retreated a step, tamping down the nerve endings that were prickling with disappointment at not being in contact with her anymore. "There are remote stashes of chemical weapons in my country that contain this poison. We are in the process of disassembling them. If one has the proper clearance, you could access them."

"How would you get it into the United States?"

"On a jet with diplomatic clearance," he was embarrassed to say. "In small quantities, it could pass for powder in a toiletry bag."

Her eyes narrowed as she considered another option. "Strychnine is the deadly ingredient in rat poison. That'd be easy enough to purchase stateside. You could liquefy it and turn it into an injectable liquid."

Rat poison? Those sensitized nerves went on alert again, but this time for a different reason. "Would it be used for killing moles, as well?"

"They're similar critters. I imagine the poisons

would have the same ingredients. I'd have to do some research. Why?"

Ivan replayed a conversation from the evening before. "One of your neighbors, an older gentleman—my bodyguard Eduard talked to him—said he was baiting traps to kill moles when we arrived."

"Mr. Furness?" She shrugged. "I don't know him all that well. He couldn't have poisoned my brother, though. That fruit went straight from you to me to Frank. It never left the house."

"You do not know Mr. Furness as well as say, Mrs. Pischnotte?"

"Mrs. Pischnotte has lived across the street for years. I've known her since I was a little girl, back when her husband was still alive. Mr. Furness isn't really our neighbor. He works for a company that's house-sitting for the Abshers. Sometimes, he shows up. Sometimes it's another guy. I've met a couple of them when I go running."

A full-blown alarm raised the hairs at the nape of his neck. "Then Furness lied. He told Eduard that everyone on your street has lived there for years. Including him." He shook his head, searching for a more hopeful answer. "Maybe it was a language problem and Eduard misunderstood."

"Or your bodyguard lied."

"Why would he…?" Of course. What did he truly know about anyone in his inner circle? Before that bomb had gone off in St. Feodor, he'd trusted every one of them. Now he trusted no one. He was glad to have a fresh set of eyes to look at them as suspects instead of employees or friends. "Eduard is new to my security team. Filip thought we needed some younger blood. I confess I do not know him as well as Filip or Danya."

Carly snorted through her nose. "You mean Mr. Personality?"

He frowned at the nickname. "Sarcasm?"

"Oh, yeah." She paced the room again, but this time he could see the thoughts running through her head, energizing her, instead of the stress leaking through her pores and sapping her resilience. "What Danya Pavluk lacks in charm, he makes up for in grouchy negativity. He has a big chip on his shoulder. He's not friendly. He's really unhappy about something for him to be so grumpy."

"Unhappy about the changes happening in Lukinburg?"

"Or it's personal. Somebody really hates your guts. Enough to kill you in a dozen different ways. Poison. You said someone shot at you. Bombs." She stopped in front of him again, her hand finding his where it rested at his waist. She squeezed his fingers, emphasizing the dire turn of her suspicions. "Maybe there's a team of would-be assassins, each with his or her own specialty. Different members of these Lukin Loyalists." She closed her eyes and shook her head as if the possibilities were overwhelming. "Or one person wants us to think it's a group of individuals who are after you by varying the means of their attacks." Her eyes popped open. "Since there are a lot of suspects with motive, maybe we should focus on the means—how these crimes are being committed. We should look at anyone who has experience with explosives, as well as anyone with access to poison, syringes, that kind of medical or chemical expertise."

"More than one assassin?" He muttered Danya's favorite curse. "Every able-bodied citizen in Lukinburg is required to serve at least two years in our military. Not everyone sees combat, but theoretically, any of my people could have knowledge of explosives. Or poison."

"We should check their service records, then. Maybe someone worked as a medic? Nurse? An exterminator? Can you do that? Do you know how to do research? Or does someone always do that for you?" She released his hand, frowning as if the idea of him using a computer or analyzing data was foreign to him. "If you give me access to that information, I could look it up for you."

"Not easily. All but the most basic personnel information is encrypted for security reasons. Filip changes the codes regularly."

"So, that's a dead end. How are we ever supposed to get an upper hand on this predator?"

He caught her hand before she pulled away. This time he was instilling some clarity into her. "I have not always been the prince. Once upon a time, I worked in my uncle's business. Growing up, I worked in a mine. I was a soldier for six years. I know how to get information. I know how to get a job done." He paused when he realized he was defending his manhood, at least a little bit. He released her hand to rake his fingers through his short hair. "Filip would be suspicious if you make inquiries. I will do this. I do not want the threats against me to become threats against you."

"Just tell me where to look and I can—"

"This job is more impossible than I could have imagined." He wasn't going to argue about this. As much as he needed an ally, he didn't want to see her hurt. Or crashing into an emotional catharsis again. "I never meant for anyone in your family to get hurt. I will speak to Captain Hendricks to remove you from the investigation and find another way to deal with the threats."

"I'm not going anywhere."

"I have asked too much of you. Too much of anyone who is not a part of the Lukin—"

"I agree with the captain. It's personal now." She crossed her arms beneath his jacket, looking up at him with the same grit he'd seen when she'd taken down that pervert at the police station. "Even if this Loyalist group didn't intend to hurt my family, they did. I made a deal with you. You didn't ask me to help because I look pretty in a party dress and can dance in high heels—which, incidentally, I don't know that I can. You needed a cop. You needed someone who could find answers without it looking like an official investigation. If I quit, who's going to have your back?"

A smile spread slowly across his face.

That faint pink blush crept into her cheeks as she pulled back a step. "Why are you smiling? What did I say?"

He reached out to capture a lock of caramel-blond hair that had fallen over one eye and tucked it into place behind her ear. "Usually, people are not allowed to lecture the crown prince. You may advise me, but I make the decisions."

"What are you deciding?"

"I like how you talk to me, like you are talking to the man—not the crown. Although, you should not do this in public. It undermines royal authority."

"My badge is the authority I answer to. If I think you're doing something wrong, something that might endanger you or anyone else, I have to speak up."

He pulled his fingers from her silky hair and curled them into his palm. "Very well. I can see you are a stubborn woman. But I am a stubborn man. You may have my backside if you wish." He knew his English phrasing wasn't quite right. He'd find a translator if she didn't understand. "But you will also allow me to have yours."

"You can't risk your life for me. I won't—"

"Those are my terms. I cannot carry a gun, but there are things I can do to protect you and your family. I will not have you fighting this assassin, maybe an entire rebel faction, on your own."

"I can call KCPD for backup."

"Your booty is mine."

Ivan felt the heat creeping up his own neck when a giggle snorted through her nose.

"Is that not the right word for your backside? I have yours as you have mine."

"It's okay, Ivan. I like keeping an eye on your booty, too."

He didn't need a translator to understand that. She'd just admitted that the attraction he felt wasn't one-sided. Good to know. The timing and situation stank, but the possibility of something impossible between them smoothed the raw edges off his embarrassment and protective anger. "Then, despite my reservations, we shall continue working together. You are not alone."

"You aren't, either." There was neither flirtation nor argument in her tone when she spoke again. The police officer was back. "Is there anyone in your delegation you trust without hesitation?"

His choices were limited. His bunk mate from basic training was the only one he'd reveal a secret to. "Aleksandr."

"Then we need to enlist his help."

Ivan scrubbed at the tension cording the back of his neck. "I would rather not."

"You need every ally you can get."

If he'd believed teaming up with Aleks had been a real option for this covert mission, he wouldn't have needed to go to KCPD for help. "Aleks…is smart and has great vision for the future of our country. But he is also…how do you say it? His mind is absent."

"Absentminded? He gets distracted?"

"Yes." She should understand how preoccupied Aleks could get when he focused on his work—or on whatever pretty face or passing scenery caught his eye. "I do not know if he could handle himself in a dangerous situation. I would not want to put him in that position."

"Then you have to let me investigate. You have to let me talk to your people, search through your records. I need answers, Ivan. Someone nearly killed my brother. They keep trying to kill you, and the more I get to know you, the more I don't like that." She fingered the badge that hung around her neck, perhaps reminding him of her oath to protect and serve, perhaps reminding herself. "They're threatening to kill a lot of innocent people next Saturday. I need to stop them."

He'd taken a similar vow when he'd agreed to become the crown prince. "*We* need to stop them. I will do what I can to get the information you require."

"Don't get caught, okay?"

He smiled at her persistence. "I will do my best."

"I imagine your best is pretty good." He followed her to the exit, reaching around her to open the door. She paused in the open doorway and tilted her face up to his. "Thank you."

"I believe I am the one who should be thanking you, Carly." He caught the end of her braid and rolled its dark golden weight in the palm of his hand. "Does your name mean lioness, by any chance?"

She glanced down at the strands he held, then back into his eyes. "No."

"Surely you are named for your bravery and determination."

She tugged the braid from his hand. One of those endearing blushes heated the apples of her cheeks. "It's the feminine version of Carl."

"It is not short for something else? Carlotta?"

She shook her head. "Carly Rae Valentine. What you see is what you get."

"I like what I see."

She leaned back against the door frame, keeping

her gaze locked on to his. She might not be used to intimacy with a prince, but she wasn't afraid of it. "Are you trying to charm me, Your Highness?"

He braced his hand on the metal frame above her head, drifting in to maintain the closeness between them. "Is it working?"

She captured the end of his tie and examined it the same way he had studied her hair. "Thank you for caring about my family, about me. I know you have a lot on your mind."

"At this moment, you are the only thing on my mind." His voice had dropped to a husky whisper.

When she tilted her gaze back up to his, she tugged on his tie and stretched onto her toes. She kept coming until her mouth pressed against his. Her lips were tentative, perhaps unsure of their welcome, but the fingers curling into the front of his shirt and sliding against his jaw to hold his mouth against hers told a different story. Ivan was powerless to resist the sweet thank-you and eager invitation. Leaving one hand above her head, he slipped the other beneath the jacket, curving his fingers around her waist. His knuckles brushed against the gun she carried, but all he could feel was soft cotton and cool skin and the sinewy flex of the muscles running from her flank over the flare of her hip. Her kiss seemed to be an exploration, and Ivan seized the opportunity to learn the taste of her mouth, as well. Running his tongue against the seam of her lips, he coaxed her to open for him and swept his tongue into the soft heat of her mouth.

Her throaty squeak of surprise muted into a hum of

pleasure as she welcomed and returned the need in his kiss. Her fingertips clung to the skin beneath his beard as her tongue darted into his mouth. They danced together in a new way, advancing, retreating. A gentle stroke here, firmer pressure there. A nip, a suckle. His body caught fire with the electricity surging between them. The slow build of heat burst into flame and he longed to back her into the door and sandwich her body against his. He wanted to learn her curves, match her strength to his. He wanted to get drunk on the scents of smoke and spice that clung to her skin and hair. When her hand slid around the collar of his shirt to dig into the tension he carried there, he was the one growling a hungry approval in his throat.

"Carly…" He tried to retreat. He wanted too much, too soon. "We are tired." He kissed her. "I want you." He kissed her again. "The hour is late." He couldn't seem to stop.

She dragged her teeth across his bottom lip and desire arced straight down to his groin, erasing any of the restraint he'd tried to grab onto. "Please tell me this isn't part of the charade. It feels convincing to me."

"Are you pretending?" he whispered against her lips.

"No."

"Neither am I." Claiming her mouth in a kiss that was anything but pretend, he drifted closer, sliding his hand down over the curve of her rump and squeezing its beautiful shape as he pulled her thighs into the arousal straining behind his zipper. His brain burned with the fever to have all of her. His heart pounded against his ribs. His pulse thundered in his ears.

A bright light flashed in the corner of his vision, shocking him back to common sense.

"The prince and his local Cinderella," a man's voice said. Ivan swore as a second flash went off from the hallway, capturing them in the open door. "Readers are going to eat this up."

Ivan lifted his gaze to drill the reporter taking pictures of the embrace, even as he moved to stand between Carly and the unwelcome interruption. "I ask you to leave, sir. This is a private moment."

"Obviously. Could I get a name, miss?" the reporter asked.

Ivan's hand fisted at his side. A smaller, surprisingly strong hand curved around his, and Carly moved up beside him. "It's all right." She pulled back the front of the jacket to reveal the gun and badge she wore. She glanced at the man's press credentials hanging around his neck. "Listen, Mr. Decker. I'm armed and dangerous. If I see that picture in the paper with any kind of crude story or suggestive headline, my boss at KCPD will be calling your boss."

If her voice hadn't started in that breathless tone, he might have thought she was unaffected by that mini make-out session. Still, Ivan wasn't sure if he should admire her self-possession or feel offended that she could get over his kiss so easily. He shouldn't have let things get out of hand. Losing focus like that was all on him. It was up to him to make this right.

He turned and called down to the waiting room. What the hell was security for if they didn't do their job? "Filip!" He eyed the name badge and credentials hanging around the reporter's neck. Ralph Decker. *Kansas City Journal*. Ivan didn't recognize the man's name from the press packet he'd reviewed on the plane. "I trust you will be as diligent about reporting on the fund-raising efforts my people are working on for your city this week, Mr. Decker?"

"You give me an invitation to that embassy ball, and you're damn straight I'll cover it. Unless you've got something a little meatier you'd like me to write about?" Decker had been fishing for an inside scoop all along. But he winked at Carly. "You never gave me your name, Miss…?"

"*Officer* Valentine."

Decker nodded and reached for his phone to type in the name. "Gettin' a little personal protection, eh, Princie?"

Filip Milevski's bulk rushed past them in a blur. "I am sorry, Your Highness." He clamped his hand around the reporter's arm and dragged him down the hallway. "You lied to me. You said you were going to—"

"Hey, if I'm getting stuck with this lousy story, then I'm going to make sure I have something to write about."

"You go. Now."

Decker raised his free hand in surrender, and Filip released him, staying right by the reporter's shoulder as he walked to the elevator under his own power. The rest of their conversation became inconsequential.

Carly shrugged out of Ivan's jacket and pushed it into his arms. "I need to check with Dad and Jesse.

Find out what you can. I'll call the crime lab later to see if they can tell me anything else."

He caught her by the arm before she sprinted away. "That kiss was not a charade," he articulated as clearly as he could. "Not for me."

"It makes our cover look authentic, though, doesn't it?" Her brusque dismissal left him thinking she might not believe him. "Good night, Ivan." She twisted away before he could stop her, nearly plowing into Aleks as he turned the corner. "Mr. Petrovic."

"Miss Valentine." And then she was gone. Beyond Ivan's reach, beyond his line of sight. Beyond any chance to talk about that kiss and the potential fallout she might endure from the press. Aleks's dark brows arched above the rim of his glasses as he ambled up. "That should have been 'Good night, Your Highness.'"

Ivan shook his head, torn between duty and doing the right thing by Carly. "Don't start with me, Aleks," he muttered in their native language.

"A late-night rendezvous?" Aleks glanced toward the elevators where Filip waited with the photographer to escort him out of the hospital. He spoke purposeful English, as they'd agreed to while they were in the States. "I cannot wait for that headline."

"It was one kiss." One hell of a kiss. A kiss that could have led to something more if the world would just leave him the hell alone. He pulled on his jacket, unable to ignore the faint essence of grill smoke and cooking spices clinging to the wool from Carly's skin and hair. "I thought you left with Galina."

"Temper, temper, my friend. You are forgetting

yourself. And the promise you made to me, to our entire country." Aleks's amusement faded as he circled around Ivan into the private room. "May I talk to you for a moment? As your friend?"

Ivan exhaled a deep sigh of frustration before closing the door behind him. Weariness dogged at his heels, so he dropped onto the room's love seat, crossed his right foot over his left knee and leaned back into the stiff cushions. "Go ahead."

"I know you have not been the prince for that long." Aleks poured himself a cup of coffee. Ivan refused the offer for a cup of his own. He was already exhausted and didn't need caffeine to disrupt the two or three hours of sleep he'd be getting. "You cannot be seen in an embrace like that with someone like—"

"Like what? Be very careful what you say next, Aleks." His friend wisely chose not to complete that sentence. "You are the one who seems to be treating this trip as if it was some grand adventure. Am I not allowed to have a few moments where I do not have to be *on* for meetings or the public or press? Carly means something to me."

"Does she?" Aleks challenged. "You and I both know she is not your old friend from the army."

"That does not mean the feelings are not real." Ivan pulled off his glasses and rubbed at the bridge of his nose.

Aleks sipped his coffee, made a face at the taste and dumped it down the sink before tossing the paper cup into the trash. All a stall for time, and the opportunity to come up with the right words, Ivan suspected. "I do not begrudge you this relationship. But there are expectations. We need our trade partners to know we are serious, and not think we are in Kansas City for you to fool around…" He took a seat across from Ivan and leaned in. "She is delightful to converse with, but she seems…coarse. Tell her to wear a dress. Tell her to at least hide that gun. It looks as though you are consorting with a gangster. Like someone from the old regime."

Ivan shot to his feet, towering over his friend. "She is an honored police officer. A military veteran."

"Even if she was in uniform, it would be an improvement." They'd known each other for too long for Aleks to be truly intimidated by him. He slowly rose to his feet to face him. "Put body armor on her and she could be one of the Lukin rebels. Please, if you must have this affair…" He put up his hands when Ivan started to protest. "I remember a prince's speech saying that we must earn the respect of the world again to save our people. I am only telling you this because I know you want the best for our country. I know you have been lonely since taking on the responsibilities you have, that you have not had time to pursue any kind of personal life. But fraternizing with Miss Valentine in public is not the image that will earn that respect."

Only his best friend could talk to him like this—could insult Carly like that—and not find himself flat on the floor. "You want me to dress her up in public and keep my feelings for her private?"

"Yes. If you must have her with you."

"I must." Ivan's hand went to the tension at the back

of his neck, which Carly's grasping fingers had temporarily dispelled. "Aleks, she reminds me of where I came from. Where *we* came from and what we have overcome. She reminds me of the strength that lies within me, which I will need to complete this job. I need her. Plus, I will not abandon her when she is dealing with this attack on her family."

"That attack was meant for you."

"That mistake does not lessen the impact of nearly losing her brother."

"So, this is guilt?"

"This is the way I say it will be." Ivan buttoned his collar and straightened his tie, putting on his princely facade once more. "Now, we have bigger concerns than my love life." He headed out of the room, waiting for Aleks to fall into step beside him. "Tell Filip to bring the car around. Have Galina prepare a short statement to release to the press regarding this unfortunate incident. And Aleks? Find me a laptop."

He'd made a promise to Carly. There was work to be done.

Chapter Six

"Brooke? Help me."

Carly got the zipper of the sleeveless polka-dot dress partway down. But no matter how she twisted and stretched, there was no way to reach the little tab to pull it down the rest of the way unless she dislocated her shoulder to do it.

Yesterday's luncheon and shopping on her own had been an absolute disaster. Carly had picked out a little black dress that apparently wasn't the universally chichi thing the magazine she'd read through had indicated. Her father had asked what funeral she was going to. Galina Honchar had tsk-tsked at her before ushering her to her seat. Ivan had been a compelling speaker, and if she was a farmer, she'd certainly be willing to talk more about selling her beef and soybeans to Lukinburg. But during the mingling with the guests afterward, someone had mistaken her for one of the servers and asked her for a refill of coffee.

About the only thing useful that had happened was the chance to stand back from the group and observe Ivan's staff. Aleks was a natural-born salesman, probably Ivan's greatest asset when it came to discussing facts and figures, as well as entertaining guests around the conference room. Galina carried her computer tablet with her everywhere, and seemed to either be whispering into Ivan's ear, making introductions, or steering someone away from Ivan if their conversation ran on too long. Danya stood inside one set of conference room doors, avoiding all conversation, keeping his eyes on Ivan as he moved about the room. Eduard stood at the other set of doors and acknowledged her with a friendly salute. Although his earpiece and concealed gun indicated he was security, he interacted with guests who came and went, even laughing with some of them. Filip moved through the crowd with Ivan, never two or three feet away from the prince.

Ivan had been kind enough to pull her to his side and introduce her to the Lukin ambassador and the president of the American agri-business group. Both men made her feel welcome enough, but she'd been more interested in why Filip had put more distance between himself and Ivan when she was at his side, and who he was talking to on his cell phone when he did slip away. And what had Galina and Eduard been arguing about before she sent the young bodyguard out of the room to do her bidding.

Afterward, Carly had been dropped off with no time for debriefing or goodbyes beyond a quick kiss. And though he said that he'd rather spend the rest of the day with her watching a ball game and eating the barbecue he'd missed out on the night before, Galina had tapped him on his shoulder and reminded him that they needed to get to the TV station to tape an interview for the evening news. Ivan had brushed his finger across Carly's cheek, whispered something in Lukin that sounded like a promise and climbed inside his limo to drive away with the rest of his delegation.

She was beginning to understand time alone, time away from being the prince and representing his country was a rare, precious thing for him. Carly vowed then and there to make the most of the time they'd have alone—to go over answers together and give him a break from the heavy responsibilities he carried on those broad shoulders.

But so far, today hadn't been much of a success. She hadn't been able to find more than basic public info about the suspects who might be threatening Ivan, and she was stuck in this stupid dress.

Carly flexed all ten fingers out straight, eyeing the strange spots of pale pink polish where her plain, stubby nails used to be. Then she took a deep breath and contorted herself in the dressing room's three-way mirror in an effort to reach the back of the dress. "My toes and fingernails feel claustrophobic. Can nail polish numb them?"

"Really?" Her friend's pregnant belly appeared in the mirror a split second before her gentle smile did. "You're a tomboy, not a shut-in. You said you enjoyed the foot scrub. They're beautiful. Tastefully done without looking flashy." Brooke reached in and unzipped the back of the dress. "You're just not used to seeing yourself all spiffed up."

"How do you girlie-girls put up with this stuff? I

wouldn't have been able to use my hands at all if the manicurist had put those tips on the way she wanted to. I don't remember the last time I wore pink." Carly pushed the dress off her shoulders and let it fall to the floor before stepping out of it. "I'd say this one's a no. If I can't even undress myself…"

"You can't wear the navy pantsuit all week." She held out her hand for Carly to pick up the dress and returned it to its hanger. "Ms. Honchar's note said you'd specifically need a dress for the university reception tomorrow. I think we've determined that black is not your color. It's either this or that cream floral with the short sleeves."

"I think Ms. Honchar would prefer that I dress in something that makes me invisible." She eyed the floral dress. "You're sure it's proper for a university reception?"

"It's flattering and has a little color without being over the top. Besides, you can get in and out of it all by yourself. That's a plus."

"Ha ha," Carly deadpanned. She eyed the open boxes of shoes on the dressing room floor. "What do I wear with it? The sandals?"

"I'd go with the beige heels with the bows on them."

"The ones that pinch my toes?"

Brooke laughed. "You've survived on the streets working undercover in No-Man's Land. You can survive dressing up and going to a party."

With a mock groan, Carly reached for her friend's hand and squeezed it. "Thank you for doing this. I wasn't sure who to call for this wannabe princess makeover."

"I'm a regular fairy godmother." A bit on the shy side of things, Brooke Kincaid was quite possibly the kindest soul Carly had ever met. She didn't know if their friendship stemmed from their opposite personalities drawing them together, or from being the two awkward outcasts at the Fourth Precinct offices who'd found themselves on the sidelines at more than one social event. Brooke hung the dress behind the vintage-looking floral with the easy-to-reach buttons. "I think you should get this one. After this week, you could wear it to church or out on a date."

Carly snorted. "I've never worn anything but jeans on a date."

"When was the last time you went out with a man? And I don't mean out with the guys to a bar after your shift." Brooke dropped her voice to a conspiratorial whisper. "You know, the kind of evening that ends with intimate conversation and a good-night kiss?"

A brush of electricity skittered across Carly's lips at the memory of the kiss she'd shared with Ivan at the hospital. Even though she'd initiated the kiss, he'd quickly made himself an equal partner, inviting her to do whatever she liked with his handsome mouth, so long as he got to have his way with hers, as well. She thought he'd given her a glimpse of the man behind the crown. He'd called her a lioness, like she was brave and golden, a woman to be admired. If he'd called her sexy or beautiful, she'd have been less turned on, less likely to believe the connection growing between them.

Yesterday's goodbye kiss had been a perfunctory farewell, kept necessarily short because of too little time and too much of an audience. But even that simple touch had crackled with electricity, reminding Carly of those private moments they'd shared in the hospital.

That kiss had been heady and decadent, the most grown-up, intense kiss she'd ever shared with a man. Despite his genteel facade, Ivan was all sharp angles and hard edges. His beard tickled her fingers, lips and palms. His jaw was warm, unbending, saved from perfection by the ridge of scar tissue that bisected it near his ear. But even more than the draw of his lips, she'd loved it when he'd held her in his arms before that kiss. She'd been on the verge of breaking down with fatigue and stress and self-doubts about being the right woman to pull off this job. She hadn't been able to protect her brother, much less a visiting prince and the whole of Kansas City. Ivan had been rock-solid, more so than she'd expect from a man who filled his days with business meetings and press conferences, and she'd treasured the unfamiliar sensations of warmth and strength surrounding her. She was always the strong one in her family—on the emotional front, at any rate. She'd never dropped her guard and melted into a man's chest before, trusting, for a few moments, at least, that someone could protect her for a change.

But Monday night hadn't been a date. She wasn't even sure it counted as a real kiss, despite yesterday's picture in the society pages of the *Kansas City Journal*. Local Connection to Visiting Prince? hardly described whatever stars had aligned between them that night. Somewhere along the way, she'd lost track of everything except Ivan and the way his hand and mouth and heat had made her feel. He could have deepened that kiss for the reporter's benefit, or to seal the believability of their cover story as reunited lovers for the curious eyes of Aleks Petrovic and suspicious glares from Filip Milevski. She didn't have enough experience to read real passion versus a guy who was pretending he was into her. She only knew what she herself had felt. She was probably lucky they'd been interrupted before she followed the urge to climb right up the prince's body and wrap herself around him.

"You're thinking about *him*, aren't you?" Brooke smiled, politely ignoring Carly's deer-in-the-headlights expression in the mirror. "Who'd have thought my best friend would be dating a prince?"

"For a week, Brooke. And it's not dating so much as…" She almost ended the sentence with *work*. But remembering the need for secrecy, knowing that even a well-meaning friend could accidentally let it slip that she'd only known Ivan for a couple of days, that she was more bodyguard than girlfriend, Carly blinked her eyes and looked away. "Ivan wasn't a prince when I knew him…before. I'm hardly going to get serious with a man who's about to go off and run his own country in a week."

"But that kiss…" Brooke had the good grace to blush at the photograph that might as well have been on the front page from all the teasing and comments she'd gotten from her brothers and coworkers. "It looked so romantic."

Romantic wasn't the half of it. Carly shrugged off the visceral memory, reminding herself not to make too much of the bond she felt to Ivan. This was a job. A responsibility. Not a happily-ever-after in the making. "I'd never fit into that world. My life is here. My job? Dad and the bros? They need me."

Brooke seemed disappointed by her answer. "What about what you need?" Then she smiled again, as if she thought Carly needed cheering up. "That doesn't mean you won't find someone else after Ivan's gone back to Europe."

Carly silently thanked her for the unknowing save.

"Point taken. Maybe the wardrobe upgrade will help in the romance department. Maybe there's an Atticus out there for me, too." The fact that Brooke's husband, a protective, by-the-book detective, doted on her gave Carly hope that one day she, too, would find a guy who'd either look past her lack of feminine charms or who'd embrace her awkward, kick-ass self for who she was. Princes with stellar kissing abilities need not apply. Time to change the conversation. "I'm lucky Captain Hendricks gave you today off to help with my makeover. Clearly, I wasn't making the magic happen yesterday on my own."

"I was already scheduled off this morning for my OB appointment." Brooke dug through her purse and pulled out a bag of crackers and nibbled on one. Carly frowned, wondering if she'd been pushing her friend too hard today. Those crackers had been Brooke's constant companion for the past eight months. "It gave me the opportunity for some last-minute pampering before the baby arrives."

Carly hugged the discarded dresses to her chest and

urged Brooke back out to the waiting area to hand them off to the clerk who'd been waiting on her. "You are not having that baby on my watch. I've got enough on my plate right now."

Brooke laughed, rubbing her belly as she sat. "Relax. She's not due for another three weeks." She waved Carly back behind the curtain, reminding her that, even though this was the women's department, she'd come out in her bra and a half-slip.

"You found out she's a girl?" Carly tugged off the slip and added it to the pile of clothes she wanted to purchase.

"We didn't want to know." Brooke raised her voice to be heard through the curtain. "That's what Atticus is hoping for, though. I guess with all his brothers, he's tired of having so much testosterone in the family."

Carly smiled at her friend's humility. "He's probably looking forward to a daughter who's as sweet and pretty as her mama."

"As long as she or he is healthy, that's all I care about."

"Are you sure you're holding up okay? We've been at this for hours. I'm exhausted, and I'm not pregnant." She poked her head out around the curtain. "Do you need to take a break?"

"Are you kidding? I wouldn't miss seeing Carly Valentine in a dress and high heels for anything. I plan to take a picture, by the way. No one will believe me, otherwise." She swallowed the last of her cracker. "You'd better start on the gowns. It's after twelve thirty. Isn't Prince Ivan meeting you at one?"

"I guess I can't put it off any longer." Carly groaned at the thought of all the lace, sequins and spiky heels waiting for her.

Twenty minutes later, with five of them spent trying to get a pair of strappy silver sandals cinched around her ankles before giving up on shoes altogether, she'd modeled lavender, champagne and blue gowns. Any one of them would do, as far as Carly was concerned, although Brooke had pointed out faults in too much skirt, showing too much skin, or looking like one of her spinster aunts.

Carly opened the curtain and stepped out in a pale turquoise gown with a beaded bodice and a simple, flowing skirt. "This is the last of them," she announced. "Which one should I get?"

"That one," a deep, accented voice answered.

Carly curled her toes into the carpet, lamenting the heat that crept into her cheeks the moment she realized Brooke wasn't alone. Ivan was perched on the back of the couch, chatting with her friend. But he stood when Carly appeared, tucking his handkerchief into his pocket and sliding the glasses he'd been cleaning back over his gorgeous blue eyes. Hungry eyes, she thought, as he raked his gaze up and down her body. Happy to see her. Liking what he saw—if she could read a man correctly, and if this man's expression actually conveyed the truth. Not everything was as it should be in royalty land, though, judging by the lines of fatigue framing those piercing blue eyes. Carly's heart squeezed in concern over whatever stress was worrying him now. Had there been another threat? Another attempt on his life? A long, difficult meeting that hadn't gone his way? Ivan revealed nothing but a smile.

"That color is stunning on you." He pointed to her bare toes. "Although I do recommend shoes. There will be a lot of dancing at the ball."

Carly backtracked from her initial worry. She was the bodyguard here, not his girlfriend. She looked beyond his shoulders, quickly scanning the store out to the double front doors, spotting Milevski waiting just outside. Reminding herself that she shouldn't let her feelings get real for this man, she distanced herself with a joke. "I didn't think my boots went with the look." There was no one else in the shop save the clerk at the counter who'd paused in the middle of hanging up the dresses Carly had discarded to gawk at the handsome, raven-haired man who'd strolled into her department. "Where's your security team?"

"Filip and the police are outside keeping anyone else from coming in. Danya and Eduard are clearing the floor of any other customers and staff."

"Can you do that? Close down a store?" Carly asked, perhaps understanding for the first time the level of security necessary to allow a prince to be out in public. She saw Danya herding a group of employees into the break room. She traded scowls with the surly bodyguard before he closed the door and raised his arm to report into the radio he wore on his wrist. Then she saw Eduard chatting with a trio of young women as he opened the glass doors and walked them outside. "Of course, you can. You've already done it." She dragged her gaze back to Ivan, hiking up her skirt and retreating to the dressing rooms. "I don't want to hold you up. I'll get changed and be ready ASAP."

"ASAP?" Ivan asked.

"As soon as possible," Carly and Brooke echoed together.

"I see. No rush," he assured them, signaling Eduard stay by the front doors. "I am yours for the next two hours." He bent to kiss Brooke's hand. "Mrs. Kincaid. You are looking radiant today. Will you be joining us for lunch?"

"No, thank you. I wouldn't dream of intruding. Besides, I'm meeting my husband." Flustered by the prince's attention, Brooke quickly excused herself. She looped her purse over her shoulder and picked up the large Doc Martens shoebox on the seat beside her. "I've worked all the miracles I can. She's coiffed, painted and dressed for success. Don't let her buy the boots." She placed the box in Ivan's hands. "They're the only thing she picked out on her own."

"Traitor." Carly watched Ivan peek at the thick-soled boots that had caught her eye.

He laughed. "They would certainly make a fashion statement with that dress."

Carly grabbed the box from him, finding it impossible not to smile as the tension around his eyes eased. "At least they're in better shape than the ones I usually wear. I was going to pay for them myself."

Brooke reclaimed the burgundy boots. "Ms. Honchar said princess, not goth chick or biker babe. I'm putting them back for your own good. You know I love ya, Carly."

"Love you, too." Carly hugged her from the side, carefully avoiding her pregnant belly. "Thanks for everything. Tell Atticus hi."

"I will. Good luck. With everything," she whispered the last bit into Carly's ear, reminding her that Brooke thought this relationship was real. Brooke carried the boots over to the clerk before pulling out her phone. Carly could hear how her friend's tone softened as she called her husband to let him know she was ready to be picked up. Eduard pushed the door open for her and exchanged a nod as she left the store.

Carly touched the stack of clothing and unmentionables that Brooke had deemed were necessary for this week's public appearances. "Are you sure this isn't too much? I got something for every event on Galina's list. Brooke made sure they were appropriate."

Ivan gathered up the items from the couch and snapped his fingers for Eduard to handle the purchase. "She can be a stickler for details."

"That's why Brooke gets to run the captain's office. Captain Hendricks thinks he's in charge, but we all know who keeps the precinct running."

"I meant Galina. She's planned my days down to the minute. She's asked that any changes go through her." Right. Different taskmaster. "I am sure your friend is very good at what she does. I apologize for being late, but my meeting with the mayor ran longer than planned."

Carly headed back into the dressing room to change into the blue pantsuit. "Did everything go okay?"

"I spent longer than I wanted talking about Ralph

Decker's photograph of us in the paper. It was not my intention to make you the center of local gossip."

"No one will question whether you and I are the real deal or not now. That's one good thing about being caught off guard like that." A mortifying thought made her stick her head back out through the curtain. "It didn't cause trouble at the meeting, did it?"

Ivan shook his head and touched his watch to remind her of the time before waving her back inside to finish changing. "Actually, everyone seemed to think it was positive publicity for my visit. They likened it to a royal wedding. Although I am not sure I like my new nickname—Prince Charming. How will anyone take me seriously?"

"Prince Charming?" Carly groaned on Ivan's behalf. "Have any of them actually talked to you?" she teased.

"Very funny, Officer Cinderella," he teased right back.

Her groan was legit this time. "Is that *my* nickname?"

Ivan laughed. "When we got down to business, the new mayor was very welcoming, and amenable to moving forward with our proposed research and agribusiness deals."

"That's good, right?"

"That is very good."

Carly pulled the jacket on over her new pink blouse and slipped her feet into the ballet flats Brooke had chosen for her. She tucked her gun into the holster at the back of her belt. Then she picked up the package of baby blankets in shades of green, yellow and peach and draped the evening gown over her arm before re-joining Ivan. "Is this okay? It feels a little like I'm in uniform—without the sturdy footwear."

"To be honest…" He leaned in to kiss her cheek and whisper beyond curious ears and prying eyes. "I like the shorts better." He brushed the tip of his finger across the cheek he'd kissed, seeming amused by the heat she could feel coloring her skin before he pulled away. "But this is more flattering than the black dress. Perfect for a luncheon with a prince."

Idly, Carly wondered if any man's attention would make her blush like a girlie-girl, or if it was Ivan Mostek's superpower to make her react to every intimate word or touch they shared. And since she had no words to ask him if he meant half the compliments he gave her, she headed to the checkout counter. "I want to buy these baby blankets Brooke was admiring. To thank her for helping me out. I'll be just a few minutes."

Ivan plucked the package from the baby department out of her hands and gave it to the clerk with a smile that made the other woman press her hand to her heart. "We will take these, as well. Put them on my account and have them delivered to Miss Valentine's home with everything else."

"Yes, sir," the clerk answered, looking equally flustered when Eduard joined them.

"Shall I bring the car from the parking garage, Your Highness?" Eduard asked. His wink to the clerk left her scurrying to do her work.

"I thought we could do something different," Carly suggested. "We're only a couple of city blocks from a really good, yet casual, authentic Kansas City barbecue restaurant. Since you didn't get to try any of mine Monday night."

Ivan looked pleased by the suggestion. "It is a warm, sunny day. I believe we will walk. The fresh air will do me good." He scanned the store before fixing his gaze on Eduard again. "Notify Filip of the change in plans. And tell Danya to release those people to do their jobs. We are not holding prisoners."

"Very good, sir."

While Eduard radioed the security team to do the prince's bidding, Ivan settled his hand at the small of Carly's back to walk her to the door. They were barely out of earshot before his fingers tightened around the bulge of her Glock beneath her jacket. "Is that necessary?"

Carly kept her voice equally low. "Have you figured out who's sending those death threats yet?"

He shook his head.

"Then yes, it's necessary. Still not sure where it's going Saturday night, though."

His tired smile didn't reach his eyes. "I have no doubt you will figure out an interesting solution."

Once he'd opened the break room door and dismissed the staff, Danya strode through the store, his eyes drilling holes through Carly. Did he blame her for the change in security protocol? Or was the man simply incapable of smiling? Maybe he had a thing against cops. Or women. Or Americans. Maybe he resented how closely Ivan wanted to tie their country to the United States. Wasn't that the reason the rebel

Lukins had protested the new government? The surly bodyguard was definitely on Carly's suspect list.

Ignoring every cautionary instinct that warned her she shouldn't care what Ivan was feeling, she faced him. "Are you going to tell me what's wrong now?" She touched one of the lines creasing his temple. "You didn't have these yesterday."

He covered her hand with his for a moment before pulling it down and lacing their fingers together. "Not here."

Something *had* happened. But before she could press him for details, she realized Ivan was slipping a small rectangular object into her palm. A flash drive. Carly tightened her grip around the tiny device and slipped it into the pocket of her jacket. "I assume there's something you want me to read on here?"

"Personnel histories and notes from Filip's investigation into the threats and bombing in St. Feodor," he whispered. "I finally had a chance to download them last night."

"You said Filip encrypted his files. How did you get past his security codes?"

"I am good with a computer." He glanced beyond her, no doubt making sure their exchange remained private. "May I stop by tonight after the cocktail party I am attending to discuss anything you find on it?"

"Of course."

"I accessed Filip's files using Aleks's laptop but had time to do little more than make a copy. I translated as much as I had time to do so into English. But some of it is still in Lukin. We can go over that together. I am not sure what is on there. It is hard to be alone. I deleted the browser history afterward. Hopefully, Filip will not know you have these."

"Or that someone's been snooping in his records." She reached for Ivan's hand again and squeezed it with a promise. "I'll keep them safe, use my computer at home so that no one knows what we're doing."

The chatter of the employees coming back out onto the floor ended the hushed conversation. Still, she startled at the grumble of Danya's voice behind her. "Are you ready to depart, Your Highness? I will follow you and Miss Valentine since you insist on walking. The police and Filip will make sure your path is clear." Carly hadn't realized how icy the bodyguard's pale gray eyes were until they zeroed in on her. "If you would be so good as to give me the name of your destination?"

Carly had seen the same distrust in the gazes of homeless and trafficking victims she worked with on the streets. But there was a mean streak rather than fear lurking behind that distrust. Still, she wasn't going to give him the satisfaction of thinking he could intimidate her with either his bearing or his disapproval. "The barbecue restaurant on Wyandotte Street." She tugged on Ivan's hand and started for the front doors. "I thought you might enjoy a sampler of authentic Kansas City burnt ends."

Danya's hand clamped over her arm, stopping her, forcing her to face him again. "You're taking the prince to eat burnt food? That is beneath him. *You* are beneath him." His fingers dug painfully into her arm as he shook her. "This whole affair distracts him from what needs to be done. You are not royal. You are not Lukin. I should not have to put up with you."

Chapter Seven

"Danya!" Just as Carly was twisting away from the bodyguard's rough grip, with her free hand poised to strike his bulbous nose, Ivan palmed the center of the bodyguard's chest and shoved him back. With a precise turn of his wrist, Ivan had the bodyguard's arm pinned behind his back and his face planted on a display table. "You overstep your duties, Danya. You are not to touch Miss Valentine again."

His warning was as crisp and concise as an officer commanding his troops.

"Are we clear on this?" Ivan prompted when he got no response beyond Danya's heavy breathing.

Carly stayed back, mindlessly massaging the five future bruises on her upper arm. She had nothing against chivalry, but what the hell? Where did a prince learn a move like that?

Allowing time for his anger to ebb, Danya finally nodded. "Yes, sir. We are clear."

Only then did Ivan release the stocky man and back away. His glance across the store to Eduard and the wide-eyed clerk dared either one of them to utter a word about what they'd just seen. Eduard nodded and turned his attention back to the clerk to reassure her that everything would be okay. Ivan straightened his cuffs and the front of his jacket, keeping his body positioned between her and Danya. "You will apologize to Miss Valentine."

"My apologies." Danya straightened his own clothes and made a token effort to stack the piles of scattered T-shirts back into place. "I am too loyal a patriot who has had too little sleep. I was not...thinking clearly... when I touched you."

"A change in plans messes with your routine. I get it. No harm, no foul." Both men looked at her with a quizzical expression. "Basketball? The phrase comes from when referees call too many fouls for little infractions..." She was the one who needed answers about what had just happened. "You didn't do any serious damage, so there's no penalty. Apology accepted."

Ivan's eyes narrowed. "I will have to learn more about this sport. It sounds violent."

As good as their English might be, apparently, they didn't teach American idioms in Lukinburg schools. She was guessing they didn't teach that hand-to-hand combat suppression trick, either. "How long ago were you in the army?"

Ivan smoothed his hands over his short hair and adjusted his glasses instead of answering.

"I could have handled Danya myself," she insisted, stating a fact, not bragging. "You shouldn't put yourself at risk like that."

"I saw you do something very similar at the precinct office to the last man who assaulted you."

Carly shook her head at his faulty reasoning. "I'm not about to be crowned leader of my own country. You have responsibilities. There are precautions you need to take."

Danya cleared his throat. "That is the point I was trying to make. I am only concerned for your safety and your reputation, Your Highness. I feared you were being reckless."

"And you thought insulting my companion was the way to express yourself?" Ivan challenged. "I will not allow this."

"Of course not." Danya's head remained bowed. "I was merely concerned about you taking a stroll through Kansas City on this woman's invitation. It deviates from the plan Filip and Galina agreed to for the day. You are to be in the car at all times and dine at specific locations we have already scouted out. Walking through a public neighborhood such as this without barricades and proper crowd management creates security variables that we cannot control. At least, let Eduard drive you."

"Make it work," Ivan ordered, dismissing Danya's plea. "I have two hours of time free of diplomatic obligations. I wish to see and sample more of this city firsthand. I wish to meet the people. Miss Valentine will be my guide. You are the one who will adapt to *my* wishes. Not the other way around."

"Yes, sir." Danya took a step back.

"What exactly are burnt ends?" Ivan asked, perhaps

trying to relieve the sting of Danya's attack, or perhaps genuinely curious.

"Smoked and glazed little nuggets of barbecue heaven." Carly smiled up at Danya, making more of an effort to make him feel welcome than he had done for her. "Would you like to join us?"

"He would not," Ivan answered for his underling, nudging the store's front door open. "It is hard to be romantic with that face glaring at us."

Danya grunted at the teasing and led the way outside. "I will make sure your path is clear. Eduard will follow in the car."

"Not in this traffic, he won't." Once they reached the sidewalk, Carly tilted her face to Ivan's, squinting against the hot August sunshine. "The Plaza is full of tourists in the summer. He won't get anywhere very fast if there's an emergency." She dropped her gaze to their surroundings, assessing the crowds gathered at crosswalks and popular stores, gauging the flow of traffic and determining the most direct route to the restaurant. "We should talk to KCPD, ask them to block off the streets."

"And draw even more attention to my movements?" He studied their surroundings over the top of her head. "Having a rigid schedule makes it too easy to find me and plan an attack. An impromptu walk and smaller security presence should make me harder to find."

"But if there's an inside man—"

He clasped her hand, silencing that argument. "Then he will not have time to readjust to the changes. His plan will be scraped."

"You mean scrapped?"

"Thank goodness you and I can communicate in other ways." He dipped his head toward hers, and for a moment, she thought he would kiss her again. She shocked herself with just how much she wanted him to put his lips against hers. Instead, perhaps because of the audience of bodyguards and bystanders, he brushed his fingertip across the apple of her cheek. Who was she kidding? She didn't need Ivan's kiss, not when she reacted to even that simple caress with an instant, answering heat.

"Thank goodness," she whispered, her voice dropping to a husky pitch. Had she been foolish to think, for any moment, that this connection between them had been pretend? The history between them might be a fiction, but everything she felt for Ivan Mostek was real.

She inhaled deeply and pulled away as another thought struck her. She was going to get her heart broken, wasn't she? In a matter of days, she was already halfway in love with Ivan. But days were all they had, all they could ever have. There was no commitment to this relationship, not when it was built on lies and danger and political intrigue. Was this her life? That she would give her heart to the one man she could never have?

Sealing up her heart against caring too much, Carly relayed the route she planned to take through the Plaza to Filip. She was here to be a cop, to be a secret protector. Ivan wasn't really her Prince Charming, she wasn't

any stinkin' Cinderella and she had no business falling in love with him.

While the security team moved out, Carly stayed
by Ivan's side and pulled out her phone. "I'm going to
call the captain and let him know our location. He can
put some officers on standby. Just in case."

"Already done," Filip declared, tucking his phone
into his jacket pocket. He jogged up to join them.
"Maybe you're right, and you can blend in with the
tourists."

After Filip headed out, Carly reluctantly put her
phone away. "How far do you think someone like
Danya would go to maintain his standards of honor
and Lukin tradition? Clearly, he doesn't think I'm wor-
thy. Would he go after a prince who is modernizing and
maybe even Americanizing his country?"

"Everyone around me is suspect," Ivan confessed.
"Danya might feel he is putting country before king
by sending those threats."

"No more gallant moves to defend me, okay?"

"I make no guarantees." Despite the distance she
tried to keep, Ivan gripped her hand and they set out
side by side. Although his team cleared the area immediately surrounding them, there were a few pointing
fingers and whispers about a TV appearance that morning from the people they passed. One brave soul asked
if she could take a picture with Ivan, and he obliged.
Carly was aware of a few more phones capturing a
snapshot or video, of bodyguards warning onlookers
to keep their distance and of friendly questions from
pedestrians they passed.

Ivan answered each request with a wave and a smile and something complimentary to say about Kansas City. No one spoke to Carly directly, although she was certain she was included in some of those informal photographs.

Lunch was a yummy mix of brisket, scalloped potatoes and conversation with a man who was both funny and endearing. Who was she kidding with the whole this-is-a-charade-don't-let-your-heart-get-involved vow? Carly was already involved.

She didn't think she'd ever tire of looking into that polished, angular face that was more interesting than handsome. And she didn't think she'd tire of listening to Ivan's sexy accent—whether he was discussing food, the Lukin economy or the dribble of barbecue sauce he dabbed from the corner of her mouth. The more time she spent with Ivan, the less she thought of him as a prince and the more she thought of him as a man. An attractive man. An attractive man who made her feel feminine, and yet who respected, or perhaps was even fascinated by her independent spirit.

The more time she spent with Ivan, the more the lines blurred between charade and reality. She might not fully trust that his kisses and flirtations were real, that he was falling for her the same way she was falling for him, but she could think of him as a friend. And she liked that. She liked that a lot.

They polished off the crème brûlée he'd insisted they share for dessert while Ivan told her about his childhood in the poor mining town of Moravska, nestled in the mountains near the Lukinburg border.

Including their military service and working-class up-
bringing, they had more in common than two people
raised on different continents with such different fu-
tures might expect.

"What happened to your parents?" Carly asked since
he'd only mentioned the aunt and uncle who'd raised
him. "Sorry. That was a little abrupt." She cushioned
the blow of the forward question by revealing her own
loss. "My mom died in a freak accident. She was carrying laundry down to the basement, fell on the stairs
and hit her head on the concrete floor. Dad was at
work. Frank and Jesse were at school. I had half day
kindergarten. I called 9-1-1 when I heard the crash.
We'd just learned that at school—what to do if there's
an emergency."

His eyes narrowed behind his glasses, and it was
becoming less and less of a surprise when he reached
across the table to take her hand. "You found your
mother?"

Carly was touched by his concern, but then shrugged
it away with a smile. Her mother's death was a tragedy
that had impacted her entire life. But she'd also come
to terms with the loss. "The ME said she died almost
immediately. Not that I would have known how to help
her. I just held her hand until the paramedics came."

Ivan's thumb rubbed against the pulse point of her
wrist. "You have always been a brave woman."

She wondered if he could feel the blood hammer-
ing through her veins at the subtle caress that was as
arousing as it was comforting. "I was five years old.
Hardly a woman."

"You took action. You did what needed to be done at a very difficult time. Even so young. I am sorry for your loss."

"Losing her so young also explains why I'm better at taking down bad guys than I am at dressing up and playing princess. As you might imagine, Dad and my brothers were never very good at that girlie-girl stuff."

He smiled at the joke for a moment before the laugh lines disappeared and he leaned into the table. "My parents were murdered by Vasily Gordeeva. He was head of a crime family who had great influence on the previous leaders of Lukinburg. Mother and Father took exception to having their wages garnished at the munitions factory where they worked to pad his bank account. They protested working conditions in general. When they led the movement to unionize laborers, there was a car bomb. My uncle whisked me away right after the funeral."

"Oh, my God. How awful. I'm so sorry." She switched their grip to capture his hand with both of hers. Then she leaned in as a frightening possibility turned her compassion to suspicion. "Ivan. A car bomb? The bombing at St. Feodor? The king who was blown up? Couldn't the incidents be related? Could what's happening now be a part of the protests your parents were involved with?"

"Of course not. Mother and Father were never…" He released her and sat back in the booth, pulling off his glasses and rubbing at the dimples on either side of his nose left by the frames as if he was plagued by a sudden headache. He set his glasses on top of the table and focused those blue eyes at her. "Gordeeva died in 2012, after serving time in prison. His influence on the former government's regime died when he did. The king's assassination happened when my parents were children. They are not related."

But Carly couldn't ignore the obvious similarities between the crimes. "Ivan, we can't dismiss any possibility right now. Even something that happened years ago. When you're investigating a case, you look at all the facts and then come up with a theory. You don't force the facts to fit into whatever theory you might have."

"Their murders are not related to any of the threats against the crown." On that royal dictate, he slid out of the booth and buttoned his jacket, preparing to leave.

But she was neither a Lukinburg citizen, subject to his will, nor ready to give up on the potential source for the threats against him. "Crime families are known for exacting their revenge. If your parents' murders are the reason he went to prison—"

"My parents' deaths have nothing to do with the threats now," he snapped in a hushed tone. End of discussion.

For him, maybe. "You forgot these, Bossy Boots. Excuse me, Your *Royal* Bossy Boots." She scooped up his glasses from the table as she stood, refusing to ignore what he'd told her. "Did Gordeeva have family? People who feel they've been wronged have long memories."

"Bossy Boots? The words make no sense to me. But I understand by your attitude that I was rude. No better than Danya." He inclined his head in a brief bow. "I apologize for my tone. We should go." He slipped his glasses on and headed for the front door.

Once they reached the lobby, Filip stepped in to handle the bill and tip. Carly pulled Ivan into a relatively private corner of the foyer. "What's wrong? What aren't you telling me?"

His chest expanded with a deep breath before he captured her face between his hands and touched his forehead to hers. "I have been as honest with you as the dictates of this position allow me to be." His fingers slipped into her hair and tightened around her skull as he pressed a hard kiss to her lips. She felt the stamp of his mouth like a brand against her skin. Her blood quickened in her veins and pooled in places that made her feverish with desire. But he ended the kiss before she could fully respond. "Please do not hold this against me. I cannot tell you how important your trust is to me."

Carly wound her fingers around his wrists to keep him from pulling away. "Do you really think keeping secrets right now is the smartest way to go? How can I protect you if I don't know everything I need to?"

"I have said too much already. You…" He smoothed her hair into place as his mouth twisted with a wry smile. "You distract me. You are a breath of fresh air in a life that has not been my own for these long past months. But I cannot forget my duty to my country." He pulled away, capturing the braid that hung in front of her shoulder before releasing that, too. "I am sorry, *dorogoy*."

She studied him intently, on the verge of under-standing something she couldn't quite put her finger on. Maybe after all these years, her feminine intuition was finally kicking in, and she was recognizing the genuineness of his interest in her, along with the re-gret he felt at starting something that couldn't last. She stretched up on tiptoe to capture his mouth in a quick kiss that didn't convey half of what she was thinking or feeling, only that she was thinking about and feeling more for this troubled prince and this impossible rela-tionship than a street-smart survivor like her should.

"We're still partners in this. Even if you can't tell me everything. Right now." She hinted that maybe he would before this week was over, although he gave no indication that he might. With her undercover work, she understood about keeping secrets better than most. Still, when it came to her personal life, she wasn't a big fan of holding back the truth. With a mental slap to the back of the head, she reminded herself that her relationship with Ivan *was* an undercover assignment, not the real deal, no matter what her blossoming femi-nine intuition might say. "We'd better get going. I won't have Danya accusing me of making you late for your next appointment in addition to forcing you to eat burnt American food."

He laughed at that, his expression relaxing into a more natural smile. "Do you know how many people are afraid to stand up for what they honestly think if it differs from my opinion? Other than the threats, they kowtow to the crown and tell me what they think I want to hear. Never be that person."

"Mouthy? Pushy?"

"Honest."

The irony that he wasn't being completely honest with her wasn't lost on either of them. She could read the regret in his eyes. Maybe that was a hazard of politics. There were always secrets to keep.

Filip nudged Ivan from behind before she could decide how to respond to that compliment. "We are ready, Your Highness."

Ivan linked his hand with hers and they walked out the door together. This time, in addition to the suffocating envelope of humid air pressing around them, a group of pedestrians had gathered on the sidewalk outside the restaurant, blocking their path.

"He was on TV."

"I saw him in the paper."

"I thought he was single."

"He's cute."

"Prince Ivan!"

Cars stopped on the street beyond them, too, the drivers curious about why people were congregating there. And although a few pedestrians walked on by, most of them stopped, growing the size of the crowd in either direction. Almost all of them raised their phones to snap pictures and videos, and call or text their friends to share this brush with fame. Others held out pens and various items like notebooks and coffee cups for an autograph.

Ivan pulled up, smiling and waving for a few pictures. A school-age girl handed Carly a flower and asked if she was a princess.

But there was no place for them to go without walking into the crowd.

Danya grumbled behind them. "I believe the tourists are now aware that there is royalty among them. We should go back inside and wait for the car to pick you up."

Filip stepped toward the crowd, pushing them back as he gave Danya an order. "Get them moving toward the parking garage." He turned to their audience. "Ladies and gentlemen, please. Prince Ivan is grateful for your interest and support, but he must get to his next engagement."

Carly wondered how anyone could possibly get used to this kind of attention when she saw a white van pulling up on the other side of the median. A man scrambled out from behind the wheel and hefted a camera onto his shoulder. She recognized the dark-haired woman from a local news station scurrying after him with a microphone. "A TV crew is here, too." Someone in the crowd called her Blondie, told her to smile and snapped a picture. She was certain she'd looked more startled than photogenic. "Is this normal?"

Ivan managed to speak under his breath without losing his smile. "Not spur-of-the-moment like this. There are other public appearances planned, with larger venues to accommodate this many people. This is unexpected. Someone must have posted to social media that I was at the restaurant."

Not anyone who wished him well. "This could turn ugly fast." She tugged on Ivan's hand, pulling him with her a few steps. "Someone could get hurt."

But it seemed that for every square foot of pavement Filip cleared in their forward route, the curious onlookers who'd spotted the visiting celebrity pushed in that much closer behind them. Soon, Carly's and Ivan's backs were against the stucco walls and storefront windows, and their path to the next cross street was blocked. Traffic was quickly backing up beyond that. It didn't help that Ivan was being his cordial, diplomatic self and answering questions on everything from "What did you have to eat?" and "Do you have a crown?" to "How much gold is in Lukinburg?"

"We have plenty of gold now that we have developed new mining practices," he explained. But either she tugged, or he nudged with each answer to keep them moving toward the street. "Our real treasure is quartz, which is used in high-tech applications, such as circuit boards and computer components here in your country." He planted his feet and stared into the crowd as people jostled for position to see and hear him. Carly understood now that he was trying to control the crowd, to keep them from stampeding or stumbling off a curb or getting pushed in front of a moving vehicle. The crowd pulsed like a living, breathing thing. And while Carly searched for a clear path, Ivan raised his voice to be heard. "Please. I am happy to answer your questions. Perhaps if we all take a deep breath."

Carly turned her face to his shoulder. "I'm sorry I got you into this mess. But we need to get out of here."

The click of cameras and phones and whispered conversations sounded like the buzzing of bees. "Any ideas?"

"I'm thinking." She scanned up and down the street, looked past the crowd, glimpsed everyone's reflection in the display window behind them. Something wasn't right. She turned, trying to make eye contact with every face in the crowd.

Ivan answered a question about the upcoming ball. Maybe if he kept talking, they would stand still and listen. "We are hosting a joint fund-raiser with one of your local universities to develop clean technology that will use our natural resources. I will be meeting with Dr. Ian Lombard and his team tomorrow to discuss this exciting new research."

"Is it true that someone tried to kill you?" someone shouted.

Ivan's smooth facade slipped for a moment. His grip tightened on Carly's hand and the crowd fell silent. Like Carly, he skimmed the faces in the crowd to see who had asked that. "I am sorry. Who...?"

The chatter started up as suddenly as it had stopped, growing louder as people shouted questions and turned to each other to voice curiosity about Ivan's well-being and concern about the threat of danger to themselves.

"Have those threats followed you to Kansas City?" The television camera caught them in a spotlight as the female reporter thrust her microphone toward Ivan. "I heard that someone tried to poison you."

Ivan shielded his eyes and muttered under his breath to Carly. "I did not publicize—"

"That reporter at the hospital," Carly seethed beneath her breath. "He wasn't after a scandal. He wanted to know what happened to Frank. He must know about the threats."

"If I get my hands on Ralph Decker—"

"Please. Ladies and gentlemen." Filip moved in front of them, his sheer bulk forcing the crowd back a couple of feet. "Prince Ivan's security and that of your people is our top priority. As you can see, he is perfectly fine." The camera's bright light swung toward him. "We are working very closely with the local police to ensure everyone's safety throughout our visit to your lovely city."

Danya cursed ahead of them. "Where are all your police friends now?"

Good question. Lunch had lasted over an hour. Hendricks should have had officers on the scene long before now. "Did you call for backup?"

Filip bought them two more steps. "Of course I did."

Did he? Did he really?

"Where are they?" Carly glared at him. There should be bicycle cops, patrol cars. She should have followed her instincts and called Hendricks herself.

But this wasn't the time for placing blame. Maybe the traitor had countermanded Milevski's order. Maybe Milevski had seen an opportunity to create chaos to mask an attempt on Ivan's life, and had never called for local reinforcements at all.

Danya shouted to them from the corner. "This way!"

But the path he'd made to the crosswalk filled in before they could reach it. "Eduard! Get the car. Now!"

"Yes, sir!" The younger bodyguard pushed his way through the mass of people. When he reached the relative opening of the boulevard, Eduard put up his hand to stop traffic, running across to the median and onto the next block.

"Go." Filip looked over his shoulder and used his head to point them toward Danya. "I will handle this." He turned back to the reporter. "If you want specific details about the poisoning incident, you should contact Galina Honchar at—"

"Your Highness!" Danya moved a pair of teenagers aside and waved Ivan closer.

They weren't going to make it. Ivan bumped into Carly's back when she stopped abruptly.

Ivan's hands clamped around her shoulders. "Carly?"

Something wasn't right here. This was no ordinary gathering of fans and curiosity-seekers. "Do you feel like you're being herded to a particular place? In a particular direction?"

Ivan considered her assessment. His fingers tightened in a silent yes. "We have no other way to go."

The crowd had become a living, pulsing entity, pushing forward, nearly encircling them, as if someone was egging them on in pursuit of the prince. All it needed was a spark of panic to flash over into a mob. Carly glanced up at the second-story windows and rooftops. They had no advantage here if things went south. Everyone's eyes were on Ivan. Who knew how many more people she couldn't see might be watching them right now? Maybe if she removed the star attraction, the crowd would disband. Carly looked back at Filip. "Where's the car?"

"Parking garage across from the bookstore. Lower level." Filip had one hand on Ivan's shoulder and his other arm extended to keep anyone from coming any closer.

And then she saw a reflection in the display window. A man who didn't fit with the rest of the fans. He wore a hooded coat, masking most of his face. He wasn't asking questions, wasn't taking pictures. And the shadowy maw inside that hood was focused squarely on them.

Chapter Eight

"Why is he wearing a coat?" Carly murmured, feeling the threat rising like the heat on her skin.

Ivan had seen him, too. "That is him."

"Him who?"

"End Ivan!" someone shouted. The hooded man?

To Carly's surprise, Ivan lunged toward the threat. She caught his arm and pulled him back. "Are you crazy?"

"That is the same threat the bomber yelled before the explosion in St. Feodor. These people are not safe."

When she scanned the crowd again, the hooded man was nowhere to be seen. "The best thing you can do for these innocent bystanders is leave. You're the target. If he loses his target, he'll move on." She pushed Ivan back the way they'd come, knocking Filip out of the way. "Cover us. Get these people out of here."

"What? It is my responsibility to—"

"I've got an idea." Carly grabbed Ivan's hand and opened the door of the nearest shop, pushing her way through the staff gathered at the windows. She pulled her badge from her pocket and thrust it into the face of a startled clerk. "You got a back door?"

The woman nodded and pointed to the back of the shop as two other people snapped pictures.

"Don't follow us," Carly warned. They ran through the store into the storage room, distance dulling the noise of the crowd outside.

"This way." Ivan spotted the rear exit. Understanding the gist of her plan, he pushed open the door that opened onto a loading dock in the alley behind the store.

Carly slipped in front of him, ensuring the alley was clear before leading him down the ramp and past the trash cans and power poles to the sidewalk that ran perpendicular to the one in front of the store. The blare of honking horns and sound of an approaching siren raised the decibel level again.

"Which way?" Ivan asked, scanning the parked cars and bumper-to-bumper traffic ahead of them.

She pulled him into the street, flashing her badge again to stop approaching vehicles as they jogged across to the center median and onto the opposite side of the street. Carly shrugged out of her jacket and tied the sleeves around her waist to keep her gun masked. "Lose the tie and roll up your sleeves." Ivan had already fallen into step beside her as he shed his jacket and transformed his look into something more casual, so they blended in with the businesspeople hurrying back to work after lunch meetings and shoppers who hadn't yet picked up on the mob scene just a couple of blocks away. Carly lengthened her stride to match

Ivan's. They turned the corner and spotted the bookstore. "The parking garage is this way."

Ivan dipped his head close to her ear, never taking his eyes off the people around them, never breaking stride. "What if there is a bomb back there? Those people could be in danger."

"Those people are safer now that you're not there. You're safer."

"I do not want to be responsible for any more deaths."

"If we figure this out, you won't be." She caught his arm to stop him as a delivery van pulled out of the driveway in front of them. "Did you notice that the guy in the coat disappeared?"

"I was momentarily blinded by the television camera. I thought I had lost him in the crowd."

Carly glanced over her shoulder to see if the man was following them. But there were too many people, too many buildings and streets and cars to focus in on just one of them. "It might be a coincidence. A lot of the homeless people wear all their clothes, coats included. It could be nothing."

"It is not. He was there for a reason." Ivan sounded certain. "Perhaps you were right, and he set a trap for us. He was using the crowd to move us toward it."

"Moving toward what, though? And where is he now?" She had her gaze on continuous scan now. "And where are Filip and Danya? Shouldn't we be running into your security team?"

"Perhaps they stayed back to help with the crowd." He tilted his head toward the man running down the entrance ramp into the parking garage just half a block ahead of them. "There's Eduard." He urged her into a jog. "Come on. When we get to the car, we will be safe. We can compare notes of what we saw back there."

Carly spotted two bicycle officers maneuvering through the gridlock of vehicles. A black-and-white was coming down the hill from downtown. Good. Backup was arriving. Hopefully, soon enough to keep all those people safe. She could focus solely on Ivan now.

They hit the gated entrance into the parking garage. She saw Eduard Nagy racing down the ramp to the lower level.

The clerk in the booth waved to them. "Hey, you're that prince on TV."

"Prince Ivan?" a voice from the sidewalk called to them. "Get his picture."

"He's not as handsome as those British princes."

"I can't believe I'm this close to a real prince."

It was starting again. People milling together at the entrance to the garage. They couldn't get trapped by another mob. "Ivan?" Carly prompted.

"Eduard!" Ivan pointed out their escape and pulled her into a run beside him. "Start the car!"

Because of its length, the limousine was parked off by itself across two spaces against the far wall.

Carly's nostrils flared to draw in more oxygen as they raced toward the safety of the polished black car. They were thirty yards away. Twenty. Eduard climbed in behind the wheel. The headlights came on as he inserted the key and started the engine.

A bright light flashed beneath the car's black hood and Carly skidded to a stop. It was too late to retreat.

"Get down!" she yelled, shoving Ivan toward a concrete pillar.

Strong arms snapped around her, pulling her with him as the limo exploded with a deafening roar. A concussive wave of heat swept over them, carrying them several feet through the air before they hit the concrete and rolled to a stop against the wheel of a truck. Every point of her body was bruised or numb from the crashing fall. Knuckles, elbows, knees, heels. Ivan's full weight on top of her made it hard to breathe. But even as her lungs protested and her vision spun in circles, Carly clamped her hands around his biceps, trying to reverse their positions and drag him behind the shelter of the pillar.

But in the next second, Ivan shifted, bracing his elbows on either side of her and palming her head, tucking her face against his chest and shielding her body with his as flying metal and burning car parts rained down around them.

A heavy chunk of twisted fender clanged down beside them. Carly shoved at his chest, hating the vulnerability of his position. Instead of budging, his hold on her tightened. "Damn it, Ivan. *I* protect *you*!"

He jerked once, and she knew he'd been hit.

"Ivan!"

"Shh. Shh." He brushed his lips against her ear, calming her fears and anger, stilling the fists drumming against his chest, shielding her until the flying pieces of car parts grew smaller and ended with a staccato of tiny fragments of metal and plastic landing on the concrete around them.

The mini crashes of settling debris gave way to people screaming and the crackling whoosh of the fire burning through the remnants of the car. The telltale warning of a car horn followed by the crunch of metal on metal told her there'd been an accident on the street at the top of the ramp. At least one of those drivers had been paying more attention to the crowds and explosion than to traffic. She wasn't sure what else could go wrong.

And then she knew. "Eduard?"

When Ivan inhaled a deep breath, Carly released the death grip she had on the front of his shirt and rolled him off her. They sat up and Carly pushed to her feet. But orange-and-gold flames swirled through her vision and she stumbled against the pillar. She felt the icy cold concrete warming beneath her hand from the heat of the fire fifteen yards away as she circled around to the other side to see if there was any chance of saving the driver.

But there was no saving the bodyguard, no chance of pulling him from the flames that engulfed the car. Carly's eyes stung with tears. He'd died in the line of duty. "Poor man."

What a waste of a good, loyal man. That could have been them. It was supposed to be them.

"He is gone!" Ivan shouted in her ear.

She startled and spun around to see him on his feet, leaning against the pillar behind her. The force of the blast must have impacted Ivan's hearing. She reached up to cup his jaw, turning his face from one side to the other, checking for pupil dilation and head injuries. She didn't see anything beyond the charred bits of debris in his hair, which she brushed away.

"The blast must have hurt your ears. You're shouting."

"What? I can't hear you."

Carly smiled at the unintended humor of that tragic moment so that she wouldn't burst into tears. She'd like to blame the fumes from burning oil and gasoline on this uncharacteristic urge to cry, but she knew the emotional letdown had more to do with the shock wearing off than it did the sting of chemicals in the air. Shutting off her emotions and relying on her training, she ran her hands over Ivan's shoulders and down his arms, gently pulling away the shredded material at his elbow to see the oozing skin that had been scraped away in their tumble across the concrete.

But it was hard to check for anything more serious because Ivan's hands were on her, too, framing her face, feeling up and down her arms. "Are you hurt?"

"I need to call this in." Was her phone even working? She pulled it from her pocket. Thank goodness. Everything lit up as she swiped her thumb across the screen. She'd lost a shoe in that tumble. She needed to find it and get moving. "And make sure there are no other casualties."

The man at the gate booth was on his phone already, calling 9-1-1. She gave him a thumbs-up when he asked if they were okay, and he returned to his call, alternately yelling at bystanders to stay back and reporting the situation to the dispatcher. A second man in a maintenance uniform had run up to the blaze with a fire extinguisher, but he was fighting a hopeless battle and had to back away from the heat.

"Carly, are you hurt?" Ivan's tone had returned to its normal volume. He captured her hand to inspect her scraped knuckles, then caught her chin between his thumb and fingers. "Are you dizzy? Nauseous?"

"I was dizzy at first. It passed. I'm okay." Her gaze landed on the smear of blood on the pillar and her heart dropped to her stomach. "You're not." She moved behind him to inspect the blood-soaked tear in his shirt. There was a one-inch spike of metal protruding from the back of his shoulder. "That shrapnel needs to come out."

"I've been hurt worse."

That was supposed to reassure her? "Do you have a handkerchief? Something I can stanch the bleeding with?"

He picked up his soiled jacket from the floor and pulled out a handkerchief. He muttered a curse when she pulled the shard from the wound and pressed the cloth against his skin. "You need a doctor."

"One travels with my entourage. He is at the hotel."

"Then that's where we need to go."

Ivan braced his fist against the pillar and watched the car burn while she fashioned a makeshift bandage with the handkerchief and her belt around his neck and beneath his arm to keep it in place. Although his breathing was measured and deep, there were no more curses as she doctored his injury. His entire focus was on the burning limo, the people on the other side of the flames and the man he'd lost. "Poor Eduard. I do not even know if he has family. Those files. We need to read them."

"The flash drive!" Carly fumbled with the jacket still tied at her waist. The material was dusty and splotched with a smear of oil from the concrete, but the flash drive was still there. It was intact. "It's okay. I don't see any damage."

Despite the sirens she could hear in the distance, more people were gathering in the sunlight outside the parking garage entrance. "The man from the ticket gate needs our help to keep everyone away from the fire. I need to find Filip. Where is he?"

After spotting a uniformed officer jogging down the ramp to help secure the scene, Carly punched in Joe Hendricks's number on her phone. Then she pulled Ivan deeper into the garage. She'd already spotted the basement level entrance to one of the shops above them. "I'm sorry, *dorogoy*, but we can't wait for Filip. And KCPD doesn't need our help. We have to go."

He tugged her to a stop. "What did you call me?"

"Didn't I use the nickname right?"

"Your Lukin was perfect." He leaned down and pressed a quick, hard kiss to her mouth. They traded several emotions in that one brief kiss—caring, relief, worry, a sense of urgency, desire that time and circumstances allowed for nothing more to pass between them. "I might like it if you call me that." Pulling away, he shrugged into his suit jacket to hide his wounds, wincing at the pain. He took her arm and followed her through the empty part of the garage. "Lead the way. Talk to Joe, and then I will call Filip. If I may borrow your phone."

"You don't have a phone?"

He reached into his pocket and showed her his. The cover had fractured like a spiderweb and the screen was dark. "Not anymore."

"I thought maybe you couldn't. Because you're a prince."

"My country is not so backward that we do not have cells."

"But security? Couldn't someone call in a threat or track you? I know some countries don't allow royalty—"

Her call picked up and Joe Hendricks's voice boomed over the line. "Valentine? I've got 9-1-1 calls overloading dispatch at your location. What's going on?"

"Bomb in the Forty-Seventh Street garage. Somebody blew up Ivan's limo. Killed the driver." Ivan tore the remnants of his phone apart and tossed it in a trash can as they hurried past, perhaps taking her tracking concern to heart. "Looks like traffic is bottlenecking. You'll need a tow truck to clear a fender bender at the Forty-Seventh Street entrance before KCPD can get a truck in here. About the only good thing is the limo was parked away from other vehicles, so I don't think the fire will spread."

She pulled her badge from her pocket and looped it around her neck as they entered the store. She paused a moment to ask the staff and customers watching from the door if they'd seen anything or anyone suspicious in the garage. The general response was no help. They'd heard the blast and had come to look after the fact.

Warning everyone to stay back and let the first responders work the scene, she and Ivan headed for the escalator that would take them up to street level. "I have the prince with me," she reported to Captain Hendricks. "Ivan is okay. We're separated from his team."

"Securing Ivan is priority one. Get him someplace safe."

"Will do." She eyed the stalled line of traffic outside the front doors and crossed the street to the opposite side where the cars were at least crawling along. A patrol officer was diverting traffic off onto a side street to help get a fire engine through the intersection. Ivan stayed right at her side. He flipped up his collar and kept his head down to avoid recognition, but she was aware that his eyes were studying every face they passed as thoroughly as she did. She wasn't sure where she was leading him, other than as far away from the Plaza as they could get. Did she take him into the nearby residential neighborhood, where there was no hope of finding transportation? Head for Saint Luke's Hospital that was only a few blocks to the north? He wouldn't want the kind of attention that came with a wounded celebrity walking through their doors would bring. Maybe, they could at least catch a bus to get them out of the congested area. But why exactly *was* it so congested? This wasn't rush hour. And yes, there were tourist attractions and stores and offices in this historic area, but the chaos had gotten crazy fast, *be-*

fore that bomb had gone off. "Sir? We had a mob scene about five blocks from here. Did Milevski call in for backup down at the Plaza?"

"Backup is on its way."

"I mean about eighty minutes ago, before the explosion."

She heard the suspicion creeping into the captain's tone. "I'll have to check with his department contact. SWAT Team Two just left the building and are en route. But there was no tactical team dispatched before that. I'll see what patrol officers were sent in."

"Check social media, too. That crowd got big and rowdy awfully fast. Without enough security on the scene, we had no choice but to hit some back alleys and make a run for Ivan's limo. We're lucky more people weren't hurt."

"You think this was a setup?"

"That bomb was no accident." They reached the next intersection where another officer was directing traffic and hurried on across. As more police reached the area, pedestrians were being funneled away from the parking garage to the same side of the street they were on, packing the sidewalk with the crowds she'd been trying to avoid. "We had no other place to escape to besides the limo."

"Is the prince safe?" Joe Hendricks asked.

Carly looked up at Ivan, who was doing his best to avoid bumping into anyone and aggravating his wound. She knew he needed medical attention. Still, he was moving like a soldier advancing through enemy territory, his hand on her back moving her forward as much as she was leading him. "He's hurt."

"A minor injury, Joe," Ivan insisted, dipping his head close to her phone. "I am fine."

"He will be as soon as I can get him out of here."

"My hotel," Ivan suggested while Captain Hendricks ended the call with a demand to keep him posted. He steered her around the next clump of pedestrians. "It is downtown. Do you have your car?"

She shook her head. "It's at the precinct. Brooke's husband dropped us off. I'd planned to be riding with you."

He punched in Filip Milevski's number and gave his security chief a sit-rep about losing Eduard, the name of the cross streets where they were now and that he was with her. She didn't need the phone on speaker to hear Filip's tirade about running off and getting so close to the bomb—or to hear the warning about staying put and letting Filip and Danya come to them. "Do you have a car?" Ivan challenged, cutting him off when she heard her name among the angry words. "Then you are not driving me anywhere. You deal with the police, and I want someone to stay with Eduard's body."

A glimpse of stillness among the rush of activity filling the streets and sidewalks drew her attention and slowed her pace. A chill skittered down her back, despite the heat and humidity and man standing so close beside her. "Ivan?"

"You do not think a man shouting, 'End Ivan!' is threat enough? Call the hotel and make sure that Aleks, Galina and the others are safe." He ended the call and slipped the phone back into Carly's pocket. "What is it?"

"Ten o'clock. On the other side of those parked cars."

When she stepped toward the curb, Ivan's arm folded around her waist and pulled her back against his chest. She was certain the curse he muttered in his native language was something blue and damning.

The man in the hood had reappeared. Despite the material shading his face, there was no mistaking the "I'm watching you" signal he sent, gesturing with two fingers to where his eyes would be before pointing at them. Carly reached behind her back, nudging Ivan aside to pull her gun. But when she blinked, he'd disappeared. Moving west, she thought. But she didn't have eyes on him anymore. "Damn it. I can't leave you to pursue him."

She felt Ivan's fingers on her wrist, keeping her gun in its holster. "There are too many people here to draw your weapon."

True. She'd probably cause more panic if she did pull her gun and race after the suspect. Plus, going after him meant leaving Ivan completely unprotected. Or worse, he'd insist on coming with her, putting himself in the line of fire. "Did you see where he went?"

He pointed to the west. "That way. But I lost him behind the cars. He had a backpack. He probably stuffed his coat inside and blended into the crowd."

Being out of uniform with no radio, she turned back to the officer directing traffic and identified herself. She gave the officer a general description of height and build, plus the hooded coat and backpack, and asked him to put out an APB on the suspect. Although she guessed that Ivan was right about the man changing his outfit and clearing the area.

"Let's keep moving." She reached back to lace her fingers together with Ivan's. "How are you doing? You're not bleeding out on me, are you?"

"If you will not complain about the scratches on your hands and face, then I will not complain about my injuries."

She halted again, lifting her hands to see the black-and-violet bruising and raw skin on her knuckles. "I hadn't even noticed."

"I notice everything about you." He touched the tip of his finger to a tender spot on her jawline. "My doctor will be treating you as well, when we reach the hotel."

Suddenly, she realized how much her body ached after flying across the concrete, and just how much worse her injuries might be if Ivan hadn't shielded her with his body when the bomb had gone off. "Thank you for protecting me." She sensed she was due for a physical and emotional crash once the adrenaline of these past several minutes wore off. But that time wasn't now. And Prince Blue Eyes needed a stern reminder about the rules of this charade. "I'm the bodyguard, remember? The relationship is for show, but the gun and the badge and my job are real. If you ever do anything like that again, I will—"

A car spun around the corner and screeched to a halt in front of them. The passenger side window went down and Ralph Decker, the reporter who'd photographed them at the hospital leaned across the front seat. "Need a ride?"

"What do you want?" Carly asked, suspicious of his timely arrival.

"To do you a favor." Decker pulled his hands from the steering wheel and shrugged. "Unless you want to fight your way through this crowd and get stuck in traffic for another hour."

Carly spotted Filip on the far side of the street, doing just that, fighting to get through the crowd. Ivan had seen him, too. He opened the back door for Carly and nudged her to get in. "We accept your offer, Mr. Decker."

Carly braced her hands against the door frame. "We don't really know this guy."

"Please, Carly. We need to see the doctor." She shivered at the whisper of Ivan's lips against her hair and responded to the plea in that accented tone. Although she suspected this was more about getting her away from the danger than getting himself to his physician, Carly relented, climbing in and sliding across the back seat. If she was far from any threat, then he would be, too. Ivan slid in beside her. Clearly, he believed now, more than ever, that the person behind the threats was getting help from someone inside his delegation. Perhaps it was easier to trust this relative stranger than someone he knew had the means to betray him to his enemies. "This does not mean I am giving you an exclusive, Mr. Decker. Nor do I give you permission to take any photos of Carly and me today."

"Understood. But you can't tell me there's not a real

news story here. Something a lot bigger than this affair you're having. An explosion and an attempted assassination? I can't help but ask a few questions."

"This was a mistake." Ivan reached for the door handle.

Carly stopped him. This time he had no argument when she unholstered her gun and held it up for Decker to see in the rearview mirror. "He'll behave himself."

Decker grinned and shifted his car into gear. "You make a convincing argument, Officer."

She gave him the name of Ivan's hotel. "Go."

As they drove up the hill toward downtown, she saw Filip break free from the mass of pedestrians and run across the street to the spot they'd just vacated. He was joined by Danya now. Both men were breathing hard from exertion, both watching the car as it sped away. Filip dabbed at the perspiration on his forehead with a bright white handkerchief. When he pulled the cloth from his face, he looked pissed. Danya's hands were fisted at his sides. She didn't have to read lips to know he was cursing.

But were they angry that she'd taken over their job to keep the prince safe? That a coworker had been murdered?

Or that Ivan had survived the blast?

Chapter Nine

Carly thanked the doctor who had bandaged her left hand and cleaned the scrapes on her jaw and elbows. While Ivan washed up in the adjoining bathroom of his hotel suite, the doctor packed his bag and exited the bedroom where she'd peeled off her ruined blouse for him to check her injuries.

With the door propped open, the white noise of heated conversation she'd heard from the main room sharpened into words she could understand. Most of them, anyway, since some of the arguing seemed to be in Lukin. Seizing the opportunity to eavesdrop on potential suspects, she clutched the torn blouse to her chest, ducked behind the door to keep it from fully closing and listened.

Galina's shrill voice reprimanded someone. "We should be thanking God or fate or whatever you believe in that the prince was not in that car."

Filip didn't like to be lectured. "He should have stayed with me!"

"And been trampled? Shot?" Galina countered. "It's unfortunate enough we lost Eduard. But if Ivan had been killed, this entire trade mission would have been ruined—maybe even our alliance with the United States, our sister city status with Kansas City. It could have thrown Lukinburg into chaos."

Aleks couldn't resist diving into the thick of the argument. "Our relationships with any foreign nation would be at risk. They'd all be saying, 'Keep your political troubles and unhappy citizens at home in Lukinburg.'"

"This is not my fault," Filip argued. "*She* altered the prince's schedule."

"And if she hadn't, the prince would have been in that car when it blew up, too."

"You don't know that," Danya Pavluk grumbled. "Maybe the bomber wouldn't have had the chance to plant the device if we'd stuck to our plan."

"What plan would that be?" an American voice asked. Ralph Decker had hung around to eavesdrop, too. The reporter had a knack for showing up when least expected. Was that luck on his part? Good reporting? A source inside Ivan's delegation feeding him intel? Could he have any agenda beyond covering a story?

"Mr. Decker," Galina snapped, then softened her tone to polite decorum. "Once again, I will ask you to leave. We thank you for your assistance today."

"The prince said he wanted to thank me personally. I'm curious to find out what he meant by that."

Danya muttered a curse, as if Decker had just made a point for him. "See? There are too many loose ends. Filip, you need to run a tighter ship."

Filip didn't bother to mutter. "Are you questioning my authority?"

Carly smelled a hint of icy fresh soap a split second before Ivan reached around her to close the door. "Learn anything new?"

More than not sensing his approach, Carly was startled to turn and discover a shirtless prince. Was that allowed? Showing off broad shoulders? Drawing her attention to a muscled chest dusted with a V of crisp, dark hair that trailed in a line over his flat stomach down to the button of the black dress slacks he wore?

A split second of heated admiration passed before she realized that he'd asked her a question. She blinked, wishing it were that easy to cool the spark that seemed to ignite deep inside whenever he got close like this. "Only that no one out there is taking any blame for what happened."

"I doubt anyone would admit that their assassination attempt was thwarted by you." He handed her a clean white T-shirt. "Are you sure this is sufficient? I can order you a new blouse from the gift shop downstairs."

"That isn't necessary. Unlike you, I'm not going anyplace fancy this evening." He took her blouse and tossed it in the trash before crossing to the closet to pull a white dress shirt off the hanger. She gasped when she saw the crosshatched ridges of pink scar tissue peppering his back beside and below the square white bandage that covered the gash he'd gotten from the explosion this afternoon. *I have been hurt worse than this*, he'd said when she'd pulled the shrapnel from his wound. If the view from the front had been stunning, the view from the back squeezed at her heart and made her hurry across the room before he could don his shirt. "Ivan. What happened to you?"

She touched her fingertips to the scars. He shivered as she traced the marks. The scar hidden by his beard was a scratch compared to these injuries. His muscles tensed beneath her hand before he released a deep breath. "Souvenirs from the bombing in St. Feodor. I threw myself over the body of…a friend…to protect him from the shrapnel."

"Just like you did with me today." She splayed her fingers over the longest and most jagged of the scars, indicating he'd suffered burns in addition to the deep wounds. "You are not to do that for me again. Is that understood? You were seriously hurt. How could anyone want to…? I'm so sorry."

With a deep, stuttering breath, he turned to face her. He dipped his face close to hers, his blue eyes focused on her mouth. "Perhaps you had better stop petting me unless you intend to make me late for tonight's festivities."

"How would I…? Oh." Her gaze darted to the bed. "You mean…"

He touched her cheek, smiling as he followed the heat creeping into her face. "If our timing was better and my responsibilities were not so great, I would let you touch me in whatever way you wish. Does it shock you that I want you that way?"

She hugged the T-shirt close to her chest, fighting to assuage the inevitable response that stung the tips of her breasts and tightened the muscles between her thighs. "It shocks me how much I want you, too," she admitted. "I've never had such intense feelings with any man."

He feathered his fingers into her hair and cupped her warm cheek and neck. "Brave, honest, tempting Carly. Do you know how that makes me feel?"

"Not exactly. Most of my experience with men comes from annoying big brothers and taking down bad guys. You're a prince compared to the guys who usually hit on me." Her blush deepened when she heard the double entendre. The heat building inside almost made her light-headed. She needed more than the cooling caress of his hand to right the emotions tumbling inside her. "Thank you for taking the brunt of that explosion and collision with the concrete this afternoon. Those marks on your back should be on me." She leaned into him, winding her arms around his waist in a ferocious hug.

His arms closed around her, securing her against him. "Never. You are becoming important to me." He pressed a kiss to her hair before he leaned back against her arms and framed her head between his hands to study her. "This feels real to me. Perhaps, like two soldiers in the thick of battle together, our bond has formed quickly. Deeply."

She braced her hands against his bare chest, delighting at the discovery of how the crisp, curly hair tickled her palms, and his nipples sprang to attention beneath her curious exploration. "There were never any soldiers like you when I was deployed."

"Like what?" His voice thickened with a husky timbre that danced against her eardrums and quickened her pulse.

"Like I can't keep my eyes and hands off you. Like I already know everything important about you. Like I can tell you anything, ask anything, do…" Her hands stilled on his warm, muscled chest. "Am I foolish for thinking like that?"

"If so, then we are both fools." He leaned in and she stretched up to meet his kiss.

But a sharp knock at the door interrupted the moment. Galina was summoning Ivan to return to his princely duties. "Your Highness? We need you out here to make some decisions."

With a regretful sigh that caressed her skin like a warm breeze, he rested his forehead against hers. "What was I saying about timing?"

As they pulled apart, Carly rested her hand along his bearded jaw and whispered her regret. "I know you're only in my life for a week, but I don't want this—us— to be a charade."

He sealed his lips over hers, completing the interrupted kiss with a firm stamp that left her feeling wanted and wanting more. "Neither do I."

Ivan stepped back, pulling the T-shirt on over her head. He freed her messy braid from beneath the collar and draped it over her shoulder. How could putting clothes on feel like he was *un*dressing her? The heat that flared between them whenever they dropped their guard and got close felt intimate, she supposed— whether clothes were going on or coming off, whether they kissed, or he simply brushed his calloused fingertip across her cheek as he did now, pulling away. He shrugged into his shirt, looped a tie around his neck, grabbed his suit jacket, then took her hand, opened the door and led her back out to the main room with the others.

Carly pulled her jacket on over the oversize T-shirt. It might be irrational, but she wanted to hide the soft cotton clinging to her skin, as if it were something sensual, protective, private between her and Ivan. Wearing his undershirt instilled her with a symbolic sense of caring that she'd never felt when she'd borrowed clothing from her brothers.

Taking in each of the senior staff gathered around, Ivan buttoned his shirt and tucked it in, running the impromptu meeting even as he prepared for his next command performance. "What needs to be done?"

Aleks handed him a bottle of water and asked, "How are you feeling? The doctor said you required stitches."

Ivan took a long drink before resealing the bottle and handing it to Carly. No one had offered her anything. "My back is a little tender, but I assure you I will make a full recovery."

"Will it leave a scar?"

"A small one." Did Aleks know about the other scars Ivan bore? Marks of survival. Marks of strength and toughness she wondered if Aleks, or anyone else in this room, completely understood. "Miss Valentine's injuries are minor, as well. Thank you for asking." Was it possible she'd just heard a snarky reprimand in Ivan's autocratic tone?

Aleks apparently had. He turned to Carly and gave

her a deferential nod. "My apologies. I am pleased to hear that. We owe you greatly for helping our Ivan today."

"I'd hate to lose him." Ivan glanced over the jut of his shoulder at her, giving her a questioning look. *Yes, there was a personal meaning to that statement.* "It definitely helped to have the home field advantage today."

Aleks snapped his fingers. "That is a baseball phrase. I have learned a great deal from your father about American sports. I only wish we had enough time to see a Royals ball game in person."

"Perhaps on another visit, we will make the time," Ivan said.

Another visit? Was it possible she'd have the chance to see Ivan again after this week and her protection assignment was done? As quickly as hope rushed through her veins, it faded. He'd probably be king the next time he came to the US. There would be even more demands on his time, more people surrounding him. She'd still be a commoner who couldn't dance or pick out a proper dress on her own. Suddenly, her entire future shrank down to this week with this man. Ivan Mostek was everything she hadn't even known she wanted in a man. Strong of character. Caring. Brave. Undeniably sexy. Even if they did find the mole and she kept him alive, their time together was destined to end. The finality of that, the ticking clock counting down to the time he would leave her, made every moment together more intense—and too precious to waste on niceties like dating and decorum. If she truly loved this man, as she suspected she did, then she had only a few days to be with him—to love him—before she lost him forever.

Ivan buttoned his cuffs and pulled on his jacket before turning his attention to Galina and the computer tablet she held. "What decisions need to be made?"

Since Galina seemed to be a perpetually put-together woman, Carly guessed that the huff that lifted the other woman's dark bangs indicated annoyance. She gestured to the man sitting on the couch, drinking a bottle of water. "Mr. Decker, for one thing. He refuses to accept any payment for his services. What are we to do with him? He has been most…inquisitive."

Ignoring the dark-eyed daggers she shot his way, Ralph Decker rose and crossed the sitting area to join them. "It's an ingrained habit. I can't help but ask questions." He crushed the empty bottle in his hands and tucked it into the front pocket of his jeans. "Mr. Petrovic and your chief of staff have been regaling me with everything you hope to accomplish for your country while you're here in the US. Sounds admirable and ambitious. Go big or go home, eh?"

Ivan turned to Carly with that frustrated frown that meant he hadn't understood the slang. "You've got big plans for Lukinburg," she explained, "and you won't settle for anything less than what you came here for."

"That is true." He gave his answer to the reporter.

"And you're willing to risk your life to do that?" Decker asked.

"I am." Ivan didn't bat an eye when Decker pressed him for a more informative answer. "Galina, issue this man a press pass for the ball on Saturday. Clear his credentials, of course. The ball is black-tie, Mr. Decker."

"I can find a tux."

"Would you like to cover our visit to the research facility at the university tomorrow? You can see how our raw materials are being put to use in building American technology."

"I'd like to sit down for a one-on-one interview with you. But I'll settle for the invitations." Decker seemed to understand that helping Ivan escape the Plaza and get to the hotel didn't mean he'd earned full access to Lukin politics and conspiracies. "I thought royalty were all figureheads. But you've got a real agenda. You've got some stones, Your Highness."

Ivan looked to Carly again. The lewd colloquialism was something she'd rather explain in private. Or not at all. "It's a compliment. He respects you."

Decker's green eyes smiled as they met hers. "That's the polite translation." He turned his gaze to Galina and winked. "You saving me a dance at the embassy ball, pretty lady?"

Galina arched a regal eyebrow. "I will not be dancing. Certainly not with you. Allow me to show you to the door, Mr. Decker. I will get your contact information to send you the press passes."

Decker laughed. "I like her. She's all business. Kind of makes me want to see what's under that starched collar."

"I beg your pardon?"

"Figuratively, of course." Decker shook Ivan's hand and nodded to Carly before following Galina to the door. "Thanks, Your Highness. Good luck with everything. Officer Valentine. Hey, if a copy of the bomb squad's report on today's incident happens to fall into my hands…"

Not until she read it first. "I'll see what I can do."

Aleks laughed as Galina and Decker disappeared into the foyer. "I think she likes him. At least, she likes being flirted with. I haven't seen her flustered like that since losing Konrad."

After Aleks's matchmaking amusement had been dismissed, and the reporter had been ushered out, Ivan checked his watch. "We have twenty minutes before we are set to leave for the Mayweathers' cocktail reception." He spoke to Filip, who was adding milk to his coffee at the bar. "I assume you have made new arrangements for our transportation? And inspected each vehicle personally?"

Filip set the cup down without ever taking a drink. "There was nothing wrong with that limousine when we left the hotel this morning. I rode with you everywhere today. If I thought there was a bomb on it, would I have done this?"

Carly wanted a better explanation, a better alibi, than the security chief's excuses. "We don't know the details about the bomb yet. It could have been on a timer or remotely detonated."

"A remote detonation would mean someone was watching us to know when we would be in the limousine," Milevski argued.

"Someone *was* watching us today," she pointed out. The hooded man among hundreds of other less obviously suspicious bystanders at the Plaza was her prime suspect. If only she had a name, or even a face, to help identify him. And if she could prove the hooded man was working with any one of these people, she'd close the case and know Ivan was safe.

Ivan buttoned his collar and knotted his tie. "If it was triggered by turning the ignition as it appeared to be, then the bomb was put there sometime after we arrived at the store and went to dinner. That's only a two-hour window."

"One of our people stays with the car always," Filip insisted. "It was Eduard's assignment until we called him for backup to help manage the crowd."

"Eduard was in the store with us," Carly reminded them. "I remember him joking with the clerk who checked us out. Was the limo unattended during that time, too? A skilled bomber wouldn't need more than a few minutes."

Filip stormed across the carpet, his cheeks turning ruddy with temper. "What are you accusing me of? Not doing my job? An attempt on the prince's life? That is treason, Miss Valentine." He thumped his chest, leaning in close enough for her to smell the oily tonic he used in his hair. "*I* am a proud Lukin. If you had not interfered—"

"Are you angry because I got the prince out of a dangerous situation you couldn't control or because Eduard is dead?" Carly wasn't intimidated by Filip's bluster. She had two big brothers she was used to standing up to. She propped her hands on her hips and stood her ground. "Or are you upset because this latest attempt to kill Ivan failed?"

Her challenge left a long silence in the room. Ivan had moved in beside her, no doubt thinking she needed his protection. Now he stood shoulder to shoulder with Carly, awaiting Milevski's answer. Galina returned in time to hear the accusation, hanging back at the edge of the seating area. Aleks cleaned his glasses, either oblivious to or purposely ignoring the tension in the room.

From across the room, Carly heard a grumbling noise that sounded a little bit like laughter. Danya had avoided the whole conversation, but now he moved to the bar to pour himself a cup of coffee. "She knows, Filip. She knows about the threats. This isn't how we ran security in the old days. We should have canceled any royal appearances until we shored up the holes in our security network. Even that day we lost Konrad and the others in St. Feodor, we'd heard chatter about one last hurrah from the Loyalist movement. But you ignored it. Lives were lost that didn't have to be."

"The prince insisted on making that appearance. To show solidarity in the new government."

"The prince relies on us to keep him safe. When there's a threat, what needs to be done shouldn't be up for debate."

"Wait a minute," Ivan calmly interrupted. "What do you mean by holes in security? What is it, Danya? What do you know of today's events?"

Danya turned to his boss, giving him a mocking salute with his coffee cup. "You tell him, or I will."

Filip rubbed his fist in the palm of his other hand

before the anger fell away and his face aged with re-morse. "There was a security breach sometime last night. A hacker got into my computer files. He has our personal contact information, so it's possible he could be pinging our phones and tracking our move-ments. He would have known today's schedule, our se-curity assignments." He shrugged his beefy shoulders. "With that information, he or she would have known where the limousine would be parked, and the time frame for your luncheon. He could even have called Eduard's phone to trigger the explosion. I know there were threats made against you in Lukinburg. I fear the Loyalists haven't honored their alliance. They followed you here to the States."

Ivan reflected on the revelation for a moment. Surely, he wasn't about to tell these people that he was the one who'd gotten into Filip's files. Carly reached into the pocket of her jacket and curled her fingers around the flash drive. Still there. Still safe. Still their best lead. Anyone else who had access to those files could have used the information as Filip had suggested—to fol-low Ivan, to set off the bomb. Ivan wouldn't admit he was conducting his own investigation of these so-called friends and colleagues, would he?

But the prince had a different confession to make. "I have received two threats since we arrived in the US."

Carly's sigh of relief was drowned out by the flurry of concern and protest from the circle of people clos-ing in around Ivan.

Danya cursed. "This is what I mean. It's shabby—"

"Why did you not tell me?" Filip accused. "How can

you expect me to do my job when I do not have all the information I need?"

"Someone has that information," Galina chided. "On all of us. Now we are all in danger. How could you let this happen?"

Filip scoffed at the accusation. "Eduard was our tech man. We'd need an expert in technology to find out where the incursion came from."

From the corner of her eye, Carly glimpsed Ivan adjusting his glasses on his nose and studying Aleks, sending a silent message to the nerdy numbers guy. "This is your area of expertise, my friend."

Aleks blinked once, twice, not understanding any better than she did. "Are you accusing me of—?"

"I am not. But perhaps you could help?"

His adviser's confusion suddenly cleared. "Oh... yes. I am good with a computer. I will look at Filip's program this evening after the party to see what I can find out."

What was that all about? Carly wondered. Ivan had said Aleks was the only member of his delegation he trusted. Was this a regular exchange between the two men? Was he using his friend to cover up his foray into late-night hacking? Had he used his friend to help him keep other secrets before this one?

At first glance, the two men could be brothers, although she'd been spending enough time with Ivan that she noticed the subtle differences in their build and height. She was guessing Aleks didn't carry the scars Ivan did. Both men had blue eyes; both wore glasses, although Aleks had a slightly thicker lens in his. Both men had that rich, raven-black hair, but Ivan kept his hair and beard neatly trimmed while Aleks had embraced his curly locks and grown them out to the point he looked like a turn-of-the-century scientist pictured in one of her schoolbooks.

They couldn't be related, could they? No, their last names were different. Cousins? There were enough lies and secrets in this room that it wasn't completely out of the question. A man would trust his family, wouldn't he? Did the two men share a link beyond friendship? Even as Aleks scrolled through icons on the screen, she wondered if Ivan and Aleks cut their hair the same length and wore the same glasses frame, could they could switch places like twins sometimes did?

But what did their looks or relationship even matter? A man was dead. Multiple attempts had been made on Ivan's life. The threats were real, and as far as Carly could tell, Lukin security sucked. "We have computer specialists at the crime lab if you want me to call them," she offered.

"No," Filip snapped before she finished making the offer. "I want no foreigners looking through my records."

Was that embarrassment? Or did the man truly have something to hide?

Ivan was insistent. He sent her the same silent message he'd given Aleks. *Follow my lead.* "Thank you for the offer, but Aleks can spend some time working on this after our appearance at the Mayweathers' this evening." He dropped a hand onto Aleks's shoulder. "I will expect a report in the morning."

"Roger that, Your Highness."

"Roger that?" Ivan chuckled. "You are picking up many Americanisms." He tapped his watch. "Now go pick out a tie that does not have evidence of your lunch on it so that we may be ready to depart." He turned to Filip, who was still stewing over the security breach. "Bring the car around, please."

Danya stepped forward. "I will be driving now, sir. Since we are not canceling any appearances, despite the threats. You are giving our enemy an unfair advantage."

Ivan nodded. "Your complaint is noted. Lukinburg is depending on us. On all of us. We shall simply be more careful." He addressed everyone in the room before they all went their separate ways. "We will move forward without Eduard. We will remember him as a brave young man, a Lukin patriot who gave his life for his country. We will not dishonor his memory by failing on our mission to the States. Any questions?"

With a flurry of *thank you*s and *yes, sir*s, Filip, Danya, Galina and Aleks all went in different directions, putting down coffee cups and checking their respective gear before heading out the door to their respective rooms to finish getting ready to depart.

Once the penthouse door had clicked shut behind them, Ivan hurried over to Aleks's computer and sat down at the desk. "Apparently, I need to do a better job of covering my tracks." He pulled down a command from the toolbar, clicked in a few places and typed in a couple of passwords before going back to the home screen and shutting everything down. "There. Filip should not be able to trace the incursion back to this computer now. If he somehow manages to get through these firewalls, and understands IP addresses, all he will find is a dummy account."

Impressive. Ivan seemed to have some skills she wouldn't expect to find in royalty. His penchant for protecting her from threats both physical and emotional? Encryption-breaking hacker skills? What exactly had his job been before being named the crown prince? Would he be on that flash drive, too? Now she really wanted to get to her own computer and dig into the files that were burning a hole in her pocket.

Carly picked up a towel from the wet bar and wiped Ivan's prints off the keyboard and mouse before using the towel to close the laptop. "Now we've really erased your trail."

"Well-done, my lioness." He tipped his face up to hers and smiled. "I sensed you would be a true ally. You have done much for me. You truly have my back. I do not know how I will ever be able to thank you."

Forget Prince Charming. This mysterious puzzle of a man, who made tough guy in a tailored suit and geek with glasses equally hot made her feel soft and feminine and important without having to sacrifice one iota of the tough, working-class cop she was.

"You're welcome." Feeling a connection to him as though they were tethered together at the heart, Carly leaned in and kissed him. She slid her palms against the tickle of his beard and cupped either side of his jaw. Swiveling his chair to face her, Ivan's hands settled at her waist. Then, with a deep-pitched sigh, he skimmed his hands over her hips and cupped her bottom, tugging her between the V of his legs until her knees butted against the edge of the chair and she tumbled into his chest.

Surrendering to the demands of his kiss, Carly parted her lips and sank into his hard, warm body. She made several demands of her own, running her fingers across his short hair and bemoaning the cinched-up layers of clothing between them. Her lips scudded across his. She pulled his firm lower lip between hers, found the point of his chin through his beard and lightly nipped him there, unleashing a feral groan from his chest that spoke to something primitive and needy inside her.

Ivan shifted position again, pushing to his feet and forcing her head back to plunder her mouth with his. He gently touched his lips to the strawberry on her jaw, then nuzzled his way to her earlobe and the sensitive bundle of nerves he discovered underneath that made her jolt with each stroke of his tongue or rasp of his beard against the tender skin there. His sexy, accented voice was a deep purr against her ear. "I will say 'thank you' many more times if this is how you say, 'you are welcome.'" Carly wound her arms around his neck and recaptured his lips. "Thank you," he growled against her mouth. "Thank—"

A sharp rap at the door washed over her like a splash of icy water. Galina's prim, succinct voice intruded. "Your Highness? We are ready. It is time."

Easing her grip around Ivan's neck, Carly dropped onto her heels. "That's…my cue to…to leave." Her lips and fingertips and breasts and blood were still tingling with the electricity that had arced between them, making it difficult to think, much less speak. "You have a party to get to."

"Carly…" His eyes were drowsy pools of deep blue behind his glasses, and she had a hard time looking away. "I wish with everything in me that you and I… that none of this stood in our way." There was another sharp knock. His expression hardened, and he whipped his gaze to the door. "I will be there shortly."

When he turned away, she glimpsed a spike of black hair sticking up from the top of his head and felt a stab of embarrassment. His trim hair spiked up in several places, mussed by her hands. She reached up and smoothed them back into place. "Sorry about that. You have to go out in public. You can't look like you just had sex. Like we… Of course, there wasn't time to… Oh, hell."

While her skin heated with embarrassment, Ivan laughed. He cupped her warm cheek in his cool hand. "My sweet, honest Carly. You are good for me in so many ways. I am filled with regret that I cannot make that wish come true for you."

Right. This relationship couldn't go anywhere. No matter how right it felt, it simply couldn't be. She dredged up a smile. "You are good for me in many ways, too, Your Highness."

She was surprised to see the humor fade from his eyes at her response. A sternness crept into his tone, as if their language difference had created a misunderstanding. "I mean, I regret that I cannot make that wish come true for you *at this time*."

At this time. Meaning, they were going to finish that kiss at some other time? A light of understanding dawned. She didn't need any translation for what he'd just promised her. He wanted her as much as she wanted him. She pushed onto her toes and traded one sweet, perfunctory kiss. "I hope so."

"I do not suppose we can simply not answer the door and she will go away."

Carly laughed. "You have responsibilities." She pulled the flash drive from her pocket and held it up. "So do I."

He clasped her hand and walked her to the door. "Will you allow one of my men to drive you home?"

Um, bombs? Unknown traitor? Knowing his delegation wasn't especially fond of her involvement with the prince? "Under the circumstances, I believe I'll find my own ride. My brother Jesse won't be at work yet. I'll give him a call."

"Was I right to admit the new threats to my entourage?"

"I think the bomb this afternoon kind of gave it away." They stopped at the door, lowering their voices to a whisper, in case Galina or anyone else was eavesdropping from the other side. "It will certainly stir the pot. Your people will be working even harder to prove their loyalty to you and the crown. Either out of pride or because they want to cover up anything suspicious. That was clever, too, to divert suspicion from you about the stolen files. Aleks won't tell anyone that it was you, will he?"

"He will not. That is why I wanted him to be the one investigating the security breach. He will keep my secret."

"I'm sorry about Eduard. And for his family. He seemed like a nice man."

"Let us hope he is not a martyr for a cause."

She reached up to straighten his tie, but only seemed to be making it worse. Ivan stilled her hands against his chest, "What is it, *dorogoy*?"

"I feel like I'm leaving you alone with the enemy. I can go to the party if you want me to."

He lifted each hand to his mouth and kissed her fingers before releasing them. "I need you to start going over those files. I am tired of people dying and not having any answers to explain who is responsible."

Carly nodded. "I'll get you your own cell phone, too. A disposable one the others don't know about. You can use that one to call or text me. And no one can track you."

"I think that would be a good idea. Thank you for looking out for me."

She ignored the urge to answer his thanks the way she had over in the chair. Instead, she patted his arm. "That's why I'm here, isn't it?"

"It is not the only reason, *dorogoy*." He drew his fingertip across her uninjured cheek in a familiar caress. "I will see you later?"

A firmer knock rattled the door and Filip's harsh

voice called to them. "Your Highness, we will be late. Miss Valentine? You must let him go."

That was prophetic.

Carly ignored the big rock of reality that weighted her down again and reached for the doorknob. "I'll be waiting for you. Be safe."

Chapter Ten

Ivan saluted the trio of men in the Valentines' living room with a forkful of cherry pie before stuffing the sweet, tart bite into his mouth and heading downstairs to Carly's bedroom.

It was strange to see Aleks so enamored with American baseball, and making friends with Carly's father and brother Frank, who was home from the hospital and staying with them for a few days while he recuperated from being poisoned. But then Aleks had always had a knack for socializing. He'd been an asset at the Mayweathers' cocktail party tonight, showing the most charming side of Lukinburg, as well as being a knowledgeable representative to help Ivan discuss their new government policies and trade ambitions with the US. Aleks had covered for him earlier this evening at the hotel, too, allowing him to keep his secrets from Filip and the others. Aleks deserved a break. The three men were spread out across the sectional couch, fixated on the televised game. Filip was in the kitchen, eating a late dinner after trading places with Danya, who sat in the car parked out front and made routine checks around the exterior of the house. The two bodyguards would swap out four-hour shifts, sleeping in Jesse Valentine's old room while the other kept watch. Galina was staying the night at the Lukinburg embassy, handling last-minute details for the ball.

They were all safe for now, the game was an exciting one, judging by their cheers and chatter, and they were all full of Carly's delicious food. Ivan was looking forward to several hours of uninterrupted time with Carly. Maybe to finish that kiss she'd started in his hotel suite, possibly to tell her the truth about how quickly she'd come to mean something to him, certainly to discuss the background records she'd been poring over since dinner, and just to have a few hours where he didn't have to be the prince. For a few hours tonight, he could just be the man who wanted to be with Carly Valentine.

Ivan turned on the lower landing to quietly open and close the door that led down to the finished basement that had been converted into Carly's private space. She had a bedroom area, an office space with a big antique desk and bookshelves, her own bathroom and closet. The ceiling had been soundproofed to give her privacy from her father's loud television and keep whatever noise she made down here from traveling to the upper levels of the house. The windows had been given the proper egress in case of an emergency, yet they were covered with shutters her brother Frank had made.

He turned the lock in the knob before heading down the last few steps. If Carly wasn't already a brave, sexy woman who spoke to everything he truly was, he'd want to be a part of her life just for her cooking. The fancy hors d'oeuvres and champagne cocktails at the Mayweather reception had been tasty, but not filling. Even reheated, the leftover grilled burgers, potato salad and coleslaw Carly had pulled from the fridge had been delicious.

He spotted her over a partition of shoulder-high bookshelves, sitting cross-legged on her bed with the computer in her lap, a pen jammed between her lips, and a yellow legal pad on the quilt beside her. Pausing for a few precious seconds before she looked up from her work, he drank in the sight of her cutoff shorts and long bare legs. Her hair, damp from an earlier shower, hung loose and tumbled around her shoulders. She still wore his T-shirt from earlier, and tremors of a now familiar desire scuttled though him. The decadence of her cherry pie was forgotten as he savored the even sweeter knowledge that that was his shirt on her, and that he didn't have to share himself with anybody but her right now.

The frown of concentration on her face vanished as she reacted to some sound he'd made. She pulled the pen from her mouth and started to shut the laptop.

"Don't worry. I locked the door." He strode around the bookshelves and resumed his place in the blue-striped chair near the foot of her bed where he'd draped his jacket and tie and kicked off his shoes earlier. "Your father, Frank and Aleks are watching the baseball game, Filip is in the kitchen, polishing off the last of your potato salad and Danya is patrolling outside. I warned my staff that unless the house came under attack, we were not to be disturbed. We are safe.

We are alone." But she was still frowning. "Is something wrong?"

She hesitated a moment too long before answering. "Maybe. I don't know." She clicked on a file and turned the laptop around to show him the screen. "This is Aleks's file. It's still in Lukin. Except for his name, I can't read any of it. But I think it's been mislabeled."

The dessert suddenly sat like a rock in his gut. "Like I said, I was interrupted before I had the chance to translate all of them. Let me look at it. Trade?" He handed her the pie before pulling the computer onto his lap. "This was the last piece. I noticed you did not eat any at dinner. Sorry, I could not resist taking one more bite. Your cooking reminds me of growing up at my aunt's. Nothing was wasted, and everything was delicious."

"That's a nice compliment. Thanks." She ate a bite of the pie, and he watched her lips close around the fork and slide off. His body reacted with a jolt of need. It felt intimate to do something so simple as sharing food. But Carly quickly reminded him of the job at hand. "Is there a translation program you use? You don't have to read through it word for word and rewrite it in English yourself, do you?"

Mislabeled. A careless mistake for someone with his skills. He should tell her just what she'd find in the file. But she set the pie aside and picked up her legal pad and started going through the suspicious things she'd already found in Filip's records.

"I was surprised to see that Galina served in the

army. She seems more like the I-don't-want-to-get-my-hands-dirty type."

Ivan grinned at the surprisingly accurate assessment of the chief of staff and ruler of all things royal protocol. "Every able-bodied Lukin, man or woman, serves two years after schooling. Then they can continue in the army, as I did, or go to university or into the workforce."

"I just don't see her going through basic training. Unless the Lukin version of that isn't as dirty or physical as our army?"

"I will put my training up against yours any day."

"Okay, tough guy. That must explain why you're in such good shape for a guy with a throne job." This time, they laughed together. "I couldn't find in there what she did, though. Medic? That could explain the poisoned apples. Admin?" Ivan pulled up her internet provider and logged into a Lukin public records site. "Please don't tell me she worked with explosives."

Ivan typed in his own access code, following a hunch. "Her fiancé did."

"Her fiancé? I didn't know Galina was engaged."

The familiar weight of guilt settled around Ivan's heart. "Late fiancé. He died in the bombing at St. Feodor."

"Oh. I had no idea." Carly exhaled a sigh. "Now I feel bad for not liking her. She's always so perfect. And feminine. Perfume and high heels all the time? Makes me feel like a slacker. I guess that explains the black she wears." She scooted closer to the foot of the bed. "Did you find what her job was?"

Nothing suspicious here. "Quartermaster's office."

"Supplies. Desk work. Hardly a red flag of suspicion. Manufacturing explosive devices isn't standard training in your army, is it?"

"No."

Carly put a check mark by Galina's name and went on to the next item on her list. "It looks like Filip's most recent search was on Ralph Decker, after he took that picture of us at the hospital. Decker grew up in Kansas City, but he's been gone for years, working mostly with overseas press junkets, reporting for the wire services. He's been embedded with military units all over the world, led a pretty exciting life. He's only been back in KC for a couple of months. He has a job with the *Journal*, but it looks as though he's only been doing fluff pieces."

"Fluff?" Ivan looked up from the screen.

"Human interest stories. Social stuff. Nothing that's hard news."

He pulled up the *Journal*'s website and scrolled through some of Ralph Decker's recent credits. An Honor Flight for veterans, a science fair winner, popular summer day trips around Kansas City, gave him a better understanding of the term Carly had used. "Maybe he is looking to be part of the action again, to break a big story."

"Like who's behind the assassination attempts on a European prince?" Carly wrote a question mark beside the reporter's name. "You don't think he'd create the problem, just so he'd have a story to cover, do you?"

"How would Decker have sent me the threat on the airplane?"

"For the right price, your inside man could have done it for him." Carly dropped her feet off the end of the bed, sliding close enough that her knee brushed his. He really should feel guilty about all the nerve endings that jumped to life at even that casual touch. But he knew the only thing he'd ever regret with Carly was if she got hurt. He blinked away the distracting thoughts, set his glasses on the desk and leaned in to focus on the note she pointed out to him. "Filip's records show Decker's been to Lukinburg. And if he's covered the military, he could have met one of your people then, just like you and I supposedly did."

"Put a star next to his name on your paper. He wants a one-on-one interview. Perhaps he lost someone important in the St. Feodor bombing. I will have this conversation with him at the ball."

"Only if I'm there with you. Saturday is when all hell is supposed to break loose, according to that picture and the date scrawled across it. The last thing you need is to be alone with anyone."

"I am alone with you." She blushed when he lifted his gaze to hers. She wasn't immune to the distractions of working closely together, either. He'd never known a woman so responsive to his voice or touch. He'd never responded to a woman like this, either. It made him want to share many long conversations and put his hands all over her body to discover every place he could touch her and elicit that same rosy heat on her skin. That most male part of him stiffened at the possibilities. But they needed to use this private time wisely. He picked up the legal pad and flipped through the rest of the notes she had written. "What else have you found in Filip's files?"

"A record of threats you've received, minus the two here in the US. Looks like Filip interviewed some of the Loyalist dissidents but didn't reach any conclusions. I called Captain Hendricks and asked him to see if any of the dissident names were in the country now." She wasn't making any effort to put space between them, and neither was he. Ivan liked working with her like this, bouncing their thoughts off each other, sharing her vibrant energy, breathing in her unique scent. "Your appearance schedule is there, right down to parking in the Forty-Seventh Street garage. Changes that were made to coordinate with KCPD, running late, et cetera. Can you tell if anyone else accessed these files before you did?"

Ivan pulled up the data. "Filip, of course. Galina. Eduard."

"Not Danya?"

"He is more of a blunt instrument when it comes to security. He has little faith in technology. But Filip would have shared everything with his team."

"Unless he's hiding something." Carly shot to her feet and hurried around the bed to pick up two cell phones from the bedside table. "I forgot." She opened a text on one phone and handed him the other. "Here's the phone I got for you. I went ahead and programmed in my number and Captain Hendricks's. It's nothing fancy, but it works."

"Thank you."

Ivan set the laptop and new phone on the desk when Carly perched on the arm of the chair and showed him the text. "The captain sent me a copy of the preliminary report on the bomb that killed Eduard. Nothing official yet—it'll take weeks to go through the crime lab. But it doesn't match Filip's report on the St. Feodor bombing. The hooded man, the crowd and the shouted threats are similar, but—"

"It's not the same kind of bomb." Ivan sat back in the chair, recalling what he could from Filip's briefing on the St. Feodor attack. "The St. Feodor bomber used a handheld trigger."

"Today's bomb was detonated by a cell phone. All the bomber had to do was call the number. Either he was watching and knew when you'd be close by, or he called when he thought you'd be riding in the car—according to Filip's schedule. We were late going to lunch and trying to get through the crowd made us even later," she pointed out. "If we were on time, you'd be dead."

"So would you."

"So would a lot of people."

His jaw clenched with the possibility of so many senseless deaths. What if Carly and his team had been with him in the limo? If they'd been in traffic? Or stopped at an intersection with people in the crosswalk? Losing Eduard today wasn't the first time he'd lost a friend. It appeared that whoever wanted to "End

Ivan" was intent on destroying many lives before he got around to finally killing him.

"Danya Pavluk's younger brother, Konrad, used to be part of the royal security team. He was killed that day." She'd put a star by Danya's name. He picked up Carly's pen and, with a reluctant sigh, drew a star beside Galina's name.

"What's that for?" Carly asked.

"Galina was engaged to Konrad. Konrad died in her arms in St. Feodor Square."

Carly was silent for a moment, perhaps contemplating Danya's and Galina's grief. "You think one of them wants revenge for Konrad Pavluk's death?"

He'd considered the idea earlier but had dismissed it. The logic didn't make sense. "Why come after me? The Loyalists set off that bomb."

"You're uniting the country. Welcoming the Loyalists into your new regime." Her mouth twisted with an apologetic frown. "Maybe Danya feels like you're rewarding them—instead of punishing them for killing his brother."

"Possibly. Danya would have explosives experience. He has advanced weapons training. And he came from the same mining region that I did."

"You know how to make a bomb?"

Ivan nodded. "A rudimentary one. It was part of working in the mines."

An uncharacteristic hesitation shadowed her features before she spoke again. "The mines in Moravska? You mentioned it once before—the town where you lived with your aunt and uncle."

"That is correct."

This time she didn't just look away, she got up and walked her phone back to the bedside table. Hesitation wasn't a side of Carly he was used to seeing. Since being forthcoming had never been an issue for her before, he didn't push for an explanation. But it worried him. Surely, there was nothing in these files that made her think that *he* had built and detonated those bombs.

Ivan turned to the last page of her notes. "I see one more entry. Vasily Gordeeva. Mob boss who used to run illegal arms through Lukinburg. Significant influence on the previously corrupt government. His people were the ones responsible for my parents' deaths. He spent his last years in prison and died of cancer." The hate he'd once felt as a younger man had mellowed to a melancholia that hit him when he thought of all that had been taken from him. As a grown man, he replaced the anger and sadness with a good memory from his childhood and then refocused on the tasks at hand— eliminating suspects who wanted him dead and finding out what was bothering Carly. He scratched through Gordeeva's name. "It is rumored that one of Vasily's last acts before his death was to kill the business rival who murdered his daughter. I do not believe there is anyone left with any significant power in either one of those criminal families."

"Unless this terroristic campaign against you is their bid to regain power."

Ivan shook his head. "The new government is too strong for that. They do not have the financial backing they once enjoyed."

"I hope you're right." Carly returned to her perch on the foot of the bed and leaned forward to rest her hand atop his knee. The same nerve impulses that had skittered with delight a few minutes ago now went on alert, bracing him for whatever she was about to tell him. "Speaking of criminals and Vasily Gordeeva... I couldn't find any record of your parents being murdered in your file. No mention of your aunt and uncle raising you in Moravska. That's why I thought the files might be mislabeled. You said they were victims of a mob hit, that the Gordeevas had influence with the government back then. Was the crime not investigated?"

That information was in Aleks's file. The one she couldn't read. The one he couldn't tell her about. He'd given his word to hide the truth.

Even from her.

"Why do you think he was in prison?" Ivan pushed to his feet. He tossed the legal pad onto the bed and paced to the far side of the room before an idea hit him that chased away all the sorrow and guilt. "Enough work." He crossed back to the laptop, found the site he was looking for and clicked on the file he downloaded. He turned up the volume as the melodic strains of a waltz began to play. "You wait on your family, do your job as a police officer, take care of me... It is enough. The rest of the night is about you." He took her hands and pulled her to her feet. "May I have this dance?"

"Touched a sore spot, huh? Okay. I'll stop asking questions." She tossed her hair behind her back and rested one hand on his shoulder as he'd taught her.

"You're willing to put your toes through another lesson with me?"

She didn't fight him when he slid his hand to the small of her back and pulled her hips against his. If their knees touching had raised his temperature, feeling her sleek curves nestled against his harder frame nearly made him combust. He rested his forehead against hers, looking down into her upturned eyes. "I am willing to hold you. Always."

Her feet didn't move as he took the first step. Ivan let the music play without dancing until she shared what was keeping her from joining him in the waltz. "We don't have always."

Ivan tightened his hold around her waist and pressed his cheek to hers, wishing he didn't share the same hopelessness about their relationship. "Then I want to make the most of any time I do have with you," he whispered against her ear. "I care about you, my sexy lioness."

"I care about you, too. I want…" Her toes curled into the rug beside his stockinged feet. But her upper body began to sway in time with his.

"What do you want, *dorogoy*?"

"I know it's only been a few days, but I want you." She glanced at the bed and blushed. "There."

"Carly—"

"I know you're attracted to me, too. I mean…" Her thigh slipped between his, brushing against his arousal. He groaned in helpless pleasure. Her astute powers of observation did indeed make that difficult to hide. "I've had sex. Ages ago, so I know the nuts and bolts."

"Nuts and bolts?"

"But it wasn't great," she hurried on without explanation. "I haven't had a lot of experience, and…" Her cheeks deepened to a rosy hue and she pushed against his chest, ending the dance, though not completely pulling away. "I don't know how to seduce a man."

Her honest confession made him embarrassingly, wonderfully hard. She wasn't the only one who reacted to a suggestive word or familiar touch. Knowing she felt as strongly as he did about how good the two of them could be together triggered an equally strong response in his heart. With all the lies swirling around him these past few weeks, Carly Valentine was one truth he couldn't deny. "Do you want to seduce me?"

"Yes." She broke away to dash into her bathroom and come back with a handful of condoms. That meant she'd been wanting this, hoping for this as much as he had. "I stole these from Jesse's nightstand. I don't know how long they've been there. I don't want to assume anything. But we have all night. And the enemy's at bay right now. No one can get in here." She paused for a moment to catch her breath. "We only have until you leave. Maybe it's crazy, but I don't want to miss out on my chance to be with you. Because I think it might— we might—be really great. Will you please say something, so I stop rambling?"

Ivan took the wrappers from her grip and tossed them onto the bed. He pulled her back into his arms and pressed a kiss to her warm cheek. "It is not crazy. I want you, too." He felt her trembling beneath his touch, but then she wound her arms around his neck and resumed their sensuous dance. They cared about neither the style nor the rhythm, only that they were close enough to feel the heat and shape of each other's bodies. "Tell me what you want."

"I want you to kiss me."

He dipped his mouth to capture hers. He tunneled his fingers into her hair to hold her lips against his as he took his fill of every delicious inch of her beautiful mouth. Her feet stopped moving and she hummed in her throat. Her fingers cupped the back of his head and neck, demanding the same freedom to explore his mouth. The music was drowned out by the pulse throbbing in his ears before he found the strength to end the kiss. Her breathing was as quick and uneven as his own. "What else?"

"I want to put my hands on your skin again."

He'd never truly understood how wickedly seductive true honesty could be. With a nod he stood back to unbutton his shirt, but Carly's hands were there, butting against his as she untucked it from his waistband and pushed the shirt off his shoulders. Her fingers trailed along every inch of skin she uncovered. A sea of goose bumps chased after every caress. His muscles quivered beneath every bold touch. Shoulders, arms, neck, chest, stomach—every part of him craved her touch. He wasn't going to be able to play the patient gentleman for much longer.

Her eager fingers dipped beneath the button of his slacks, yet she hesitated at his belt buckle to lift her gaze to his. "Shouldn't you be telling me what you want, too?"

He curved his fingers over hers, guiding her to undo the belt and gently unzip his pants. "Trust me, I am enjoying every moment of this seduction."

"I'm doing it right?"

"Yes, my love." The desire that flushed her skin when she freed him nearly undid him. "Yes."

"Will you...undress me?"

Classical music swelled in the background as he peeled the T-shirt over her head and dropped her cut-offs and panties to the floor. As she stepped out of them, he pressed a kiss to her inner thigh. When he felt her shiver, he pressed another kiss to her weepy center, testing her readiness for him. Carly braced her hands against his shoulders, moaning with pleasure. "Your beard...tick...tickles there." He palmed her bottom and kissed her again, loving the grasp of her fingers digging into his shoulders as she came against his mouth. "Ivan. Please. I want..."

Ivan smiled and stood, shucking the rest of his own clothes before unhooking her bra and covering her small, responsive breasts with his hands. He angled one up to his mouth and laved the rigid tip with his tongue. "Tell me what you want, *dorogoy*."

He was amused that she struggled to speak, but then found himself robbed of words when she tugged him toward the bed. They tumbled onto the quilt, the music long forgotten as this new dance consumed them.

Her hand boldly gripped his arousal and he growled his desire against the curve of her breast.

"Ivan? I don't understand."

Lukin. He'd used Lukin. He paraphrased his need

in English. "You have a beautiful body. I want to be inside you. Do you understand what I am saying?" He grabbed the nearest foil packet and tore it open to sheathe himself. "Out loud. Say it. Say you want this, too."

"I want this. I want you. Now."

She swept her arms across the bed, clearing a place for them, tossing aside the legal pad with her notes. A moment of clarity and conscience pierced the haze of wanting Carly that filled his brain. He swung his legs off the bed and sat up. "There is something I need to tell you... You are so honest with me. I must..."

She pressed her fingers to his lips, shushing him. "No more words."

"I am not who you think I am."

"I feel everything I need to know about you. I don't want to waste another moment on anything but this." She climbed into his lap and slid herself over him. The pleasure of their connection robbed him of breath. Her body was magnificent. Tight. Warm. Perfect. "This feels so right, I want to scream. You're sure you locked that door?"

I feel everything I need to know.

"I am sure." Ivan moved inside her. He anchored her with one hand on her sweet, sweet bottom and the other fisted in her hair. He claimed her mouth in a kiss that muffled her scream as she climaxed around him. And while the aftershocks of her release still caressed him, he buried his face in the juncture of her neck and shoulder and squeezed her lithe body tightly to his, hiding the noise of his own completion before collapsing onto the quilt with Carly still snugged in his arms.

He'd never been this satisfied before. He wanted more. He wanted forever to feel like this.

But he was spent, and Carly had fallen, limp, on top of him. They lay there like that for several minutes, his fingers gently stroking up and down her spine until her skin cooled and she rolled onto the quilt beside him. "That was…" Her gaze locked on to his and her lips curved in a drowsy smile. "I knew we'd be great."

He nodded, understanding that there were no words to adequately express the connection they shared. He leaned over to give her swollen lips a quick kiss. "Never doubt your powers of seduction. I will treasure this night always."

"Me, too." She yawned, and her eyes drifted shut, breaking the connection between them.

Ivan slipped out of bed and went into the bathroom to clean up. When he returned, the only light left on was a dim lamp beside the bed. Carly had crawled under the covers and curled up with her pillow. Ivan took a mental snapshot of this serenely tender moment before slipping beneath the covers beside her. He spooned against her back, sliding one arm beneath her cheek and wrapping the other around her waist. He pulled that luscious fall of hair away from her bruised jaw and gently kissed her cheek before settling onto the pillow.

He couldn't remember a time when he hadn't been intrigued by this woman, when he hadn't trusted her to have his back, when he hadn't wanted to be with her like this. He knew Carly Valentine, deep in his soul. He would never know another woman like her. He pressed his lips into her hair and whispered, *"Obicham te, dorogoy."*

There. He'd said it. He'd admitted it to himself. To all the world. To Carly.

Only she was already fast asleep, snoring softly against his biceps, content in the perfection of this moment together.

I love you.

Chapter Eleven

Tonight, Prince Ivan was supposed to die.

The thought of losing the man who could never really be hers made Carly almost physically sick. She'd never really thought about what falling in love would be like for her, or what kind of man would capture her heart. But the moment she'd seen those piercing blue eyes sizing her up at KCPD headquarters, she'd felt a magnetic attraction to Ivan Mostek. From that evening at the house when he'd given her her first dance lesson and then anchored her in the storm of emotions that had buffeted her after Frank had been poisoned, she'd opened her heart to him. Every moment since then, through the danger and the kisses, the laughter and the long conversations, she'd been falling in love. It had happened too fast for her to realize it until last night when she finally understood that whatever was happening between them was completely mutual. She wasn't a convenient fling or a fake girlfriend. Ivan loved her, too. She was as certain of that as her sketchy knowledge of this whole man-woman thing allowed her to be.

She'd fallen in love with a prince. A relationship that could never work.

But even more heartbreaking than knowing he'd be leaving the country tomorrow was the idea that someone wanted him to leave in a coffin.

That wasn't going to happen. She wouldn't allow that to happen. They might have to go their separate ways because of politics and distance. But nobody was going to *take* him from her.

So Carly smiled and played her part. She'd love Ivan as hard as she could for the short time they had left before she put him on that plane home to Lukinburg tomorrow.

The music had stopped for now, and Carly stood on the steps at the edge of the dais, scanning the guests in sleek black suits and colorful gowns for anything suspicious.

Waiters moved discreetly through the tables at either end of the massive ballroom carrying trays with flutes of champagne. Couples and groups of friends had stopped dancing and chatting to look to the podium in front of the orchestra. A wall of glass doors framed in handcrafted wrought iron led onto a wide veranda of gray marble. Uniformed security guards patrolled out there, while several more embassy security staff in black tuxedos and utility shoes stood at each interior entryway. She recognized two of the waiters as KCPD officers in disguise, and knew Joe Hendricks, a SWAT team and more patrol officers watched the gate, parking area and streets beyond the Lukinburg embassy.

The crystal chandeliers had been dimmed to spotlight the handsome man speaking there, thanking their hosts, the guests and donors, sharing his excitement over the prosperous future Lukinburg and Kansas City would share. He looked a little more robust than usual this evening, since he wore a flak vest underneath his tuxedo. But only she and the security team who had fitted him with the extra protection would know that. She spotted the Lukin ambassador, the mayor, Chief of Police Mitch Taylor, the university president and numerous other political and society dignitaries around the room.

Their known suspects were there, too. Filip Milevski, standing in front of the podium, his hands folded in front of his bulky chest, his eyes skimming the audience. Galina Honchar stood on the steps on the opposite side of the stage, looking stunning in her glittery black gown, holding her omnipresent computer tablet down in the folds of her skirt. Danya paced at the back of the room, moving from the archway of one wing to the other and back. His barrel chest indicated he was wearing body armor beneath his tux, and his expression indicated he'd rather be anyplace but at this party tonight. It took a bit more searching to locate Aleks in the middle of the crowd, grinning from ear to ear as the blonde on his arm whispered something in his ear that amused him. Ralph Decker had left the gathering of reporters filming and jotting notes about the prince's speech and waited at the base of the far steps near the railing where Galina stood. She could see his lips moving as he whispered something to the dark-haired woman, then he muttered something else when Galina waved him away, no doubt warning him to be quiet and leave her alone while she worked the party and listened to the speech. Interesting. Was Decker hitting on Galina? Probing her for answers to his questions? Or relaying some other bit of information about the danger waiting to strike tonight?

If only she could read lips, Carly thought. No, if only she could read minds. Then she'd be able to tell exactly who wanted Ivan dead. Surely, his enemy was plotting even now—counting down to the grand gesture that could kill countless innocent people, or savoring an intricate plan that was already playing out behind the scenes.

The full, flowy skirt of Carly's turquoise gown had been fun to dance in when Ivan had twirled her across the inlaid walnut floor for the opening waltz. But the fitted body girdle she wore underneath was squeezing the air from her lungs, and the holster strapped to her thigh was chafing. The sparkly heels she wore were beautiful to look at, but the three-inch heels were wreaking havoc on her calf muscles and pinching all sensation out of her little toes.

She pulled her cell phone out of her matching sparkly purse and texted Captain Hendricks.

Nothing suspicious.

He texted back, vibrating her silent phone.

Yet. Keep your eyes open and stay close to Ivan. At the first sign of trouble, get him to the safety of the SWAT van. We'll take it from there.

Carly texted back a Yes, sir, and tucked her phone back into the tiny purse she carried.

The ballroom erupted with applause at the end of Ivan's speech.

When she raised her hands to clap, she stopped. Ivan smiled and waved to the guests, but when he looked at her, those piercing blue eyes were sending her a silent message. Oh, hell. This was happening. Right now.

A slight shake of his head kept her from going to him. Instead, he swiped the notes he'd used off the podium and strode across the stage. He took her by the arm and led her down the stairs, pushing the crumpled paper into her hand as he turned his back to the audience to keep anyone from seeing what she was looking at. "It was on the podium when I got there."

"But the ambassador—"

"His notes were sitting on top of mine. Clearly, he did not see it. When I pulled my cards out, it was there."

Carly unfolded what she now realized was a crumpled photograph. It was the same picture of the late king's draped coffin, with a very precise message scrawled across the image. *Ticktock, Ivan. You've failed. Time to pay for your mistakes.*

Carly peeked around Ivan's shoulder, scoping out the room to locate their suspects again. Dr. Lombard from the university was at the podium, sharing a few words about how excited they were to have Lukinburg's support for their research. The ambassador who'd introduced both speakers shook his hand and thanked their guests before inviting everyone to enjoy the rest of the evening, including the special wines and dishes shipped in from Lukinburg for tonight's event.

Ivan stuffed the message in his pocket and faced the crowd, too. "Anyone could have put it there. Aleks helped me write my remarks. Galina put my notes on the podium. Filip and Danya checked the entire stage before the evening began."

The audience was applauding and the orchestra playing again as business was concluded and the festivities resumed. "He's here. He knows you have this. He's probably watching you right now to gauge your reaction."

"I had hoped our killer would lose his nerve."

"Not likely. He's probably getting off on the spectacle an attack would cause tonight."

"And there are too many places where he could hide, even among all these people."

"You've made your speech." Carly squeezed his hand and tugged him toward the nearest archway. "Will you let me take you home now? Or back to the hotel?"

He planted his feet, turning her into his arms and whirling her onto the dance floor instead. Carly put her hands where she was supposed to and kept her eyes peeled for anyone more interested in them than they should be while Ivan whispered into her ear. "I cannot leave. I may be the only one who can prevent everyone from panicking if this goes wrong."

"Goes wrong? Of course, it's going to go wrong." She stumbled over his shoe, silently cursing her strappy sandals. "We should be moving you to a safe location, clearing this building and looking for a bomb."

He tightened his grip at her waist and spun her into the heart of the dance floor. "You are right. We will look for the bomb."

Once they reached the other side of the dance floor, Ivan released her waist and grabbed her hand to lead her through the glass doors onto the veranda. The night air was still sticky with the summer heat, so there were few people outside—only a pair of men smoking near the far end of the surrounding stone wall, and a guard walking through the yard between the veranda and the iron bars that marked the edge of embassy property.

Thinking he'd brought her outside for the relative quiet and privacy, she was surprised when he kept moving across the granite paving stones toward the stairs down into the grass. "Where are we going?"

"The last explosion was a car bomb. We should check the parking lot."

This time, Carly planted her feet, stopping at the top of the stairs. "No." She pulled out her cell phone again. "I'll text Captain Hendricks and have his men begin the search. You need to stay as far away as possible from anything that goes boom."

Ivan closed his hand over hers to stop her. "How many people in there do you think have cell phones?"

The last bomb had been triggered by a cell. Carly looked through the windows to the swaying mass of humanity inside the ballroom. She inhaled a steadying breath at the enormity of what they were up against. "You think there's anyone here who *doesn't* have one?"

"For the last time, leave me alone." Carly and Ivan both turned toward the shrill tone in the woman's whis-

pered voice to see Galina tugging against the grip of
Ralph Decker's hand on her wrist as the two hurried
out the far door. "I am not going anywhere with you."

Decker released her and put his hands up in surrender. With a noisy harrumph and a nod toward Ivan,
she hurried down the steps and disappeared along the
walkway around the corner of the building.

Keeping Carly's hand in his, Ivan took a step toward
the reporter. "Are you annoying the lady, Mr. Decker?"

The dark-haired man shook his head as if he was
baffled by Galina's behavior. "She must have a hot date
with somebody. And it isn't me."

"I don't think she's interested in seeing anyone right
now," Carly gently pointed out. "Did you know she
was engaged to be married? Her fiancé was killed just
three months ago."

Decker swore, his remorse evident as his cocky attitude disappeared. "I didn't know. I thought my charm
wasn't working. I'll track her down later to apologize."
He tapped the camera hanging around his neck. "Hey,
since you're here, how about a picture of the two of
you together? Dancing in the moonlight. With your
permission, of course."

"Of course." Ivan turned Carly into his arms again
and posed for the camera. She realized he was acting
as if everything was normal—that there was no threat
in his pocket, no bomb to be found—so that Decker
wouldn't be suspicious and start asking questions.

He did, anyway. But not the ones Carly had expected. "Did you mean what you said in your speech,
Your Highness? The materials Lukinburg is supplying

the research team will revolutionize the way our country fights a war? Better technology? Fewer casualties?"

Ivan draped his arm around her shoulders for another shot. "There are also other, nonmilitary applications, but that is my hope."

"Then that's a good thing." With a rueful smile, Decker shook the prince's hand and nodded to Carly. "You two enjoy the rest of your evening. If you'll excuse me. I need to find Ms. Honchar."

"That was a weird conversation."

Ivan agreed. "I have a feeling Mr. Decker is a man of many secrets."

They were still standing at the top of the stairs when the glass door opened and closed, momentarily filling the air with strains of orchestral music. Carly leaned into Ivan's chest. "Is it wrong of me to think of the other nights every time I hear classical music playing?"

He laughed. "I think of it every moment."

"I wish…"

"I know. I wish we had more time."

"There are so many reasons why we would never work."

"And one very important reason why we would." He pressed a kiss to her temple and Carly hugged him around the waist.

Feeling the bulk of his protective vest instead of the warmth of his body reminded Carly how foolish she was to put her heart before the job at hand. She was pulling away when she saw the hooded figure moving near the hedge lining the wrought-iron fence. "Ivan."

Hiking up her skirt, Carly ran down the steps in

pursuit. But the moment she stepped off the flagstone walk, her heel sank into the grass and mud, halting her momentum and pitching her forward. "These shoes!"

She would have landed flat on her face, but Ivan was there to catch her. "Carly, wait. We don't know what he's up to."

Leaning on his arm, she sucked the ruined heel out of the mud and stepped back onto the walkway. But when she looked to the hedges again, the cloaked figure had disappeared. She saw the guard several yards farther along the fence, heading in the opposite direction. He'd never even heard the figure to turn around. "Where did he go?" She turned toward the driveway and parking lot beyond that. "The guards will stop him at the gate, right? I didn't imagine him, did I?"

"I saw him, too." Ivan pulled her back up the steps, hurrying toward the veranda doors and reentering the ballroom. "Where is Aleks?"

She had a more important question. "Where's your security team?"

"There." He pointed out Filip moving through the room toward the front hallway. He was talking to someone on his radio. "Hopefully, the guards outside will have detained the man in the hood and called it in."

She scanned the room for Danya, but he was nowhere to be found. "If the intruder was leaving, that means he's already put his plan into play. A bomb or whatever he intends to do tonight."

"You get to Captain Hendricks." Ivan nudged her toward the exit where Filip had disappeared. "I have to find Aleks."

Carly caught his hand and stopped him. "You aren't going anywhere without me. I'm your last line of defense, remember?"

"Fine. Then walk with me."

They circled the perimeter of the tables and guests, pausing to acknowledge someone when greeted, but otherwise moving as quickly as they could. The music that had sounded like a tender memory a moment ago now seemed inordinately loud, to the point that Carly raised her voice. "How many people do you think are here?"

"Two hundred? Three hundred?"

Galina appeared in the nearby archway, surveying the room until she saw them. She hurried across the dance floor, her dark eyes rimmed by tears, her tone panicked. "Your Highness. Officer Valentine. Please. I must show you something." Turning back several times to make sure they were following, Galina led them back into the quieter private hallway from where she'd appeared. She opened the first door just through the archway into a well-appointed office lined with walnut paneling and gold brocade drapes. "I needed a moment to myself to review the guest list and…"

"It's okay, Galina." Carly reached out and squeezed the other woman's hand. "I could tell Mr. Decker upset you. He didn't know about your late fiancé. I'm sure he didn't mean to dredge up any bad memories. Did you find a tissue?"

Instead of being grateful for the concern, Galina burst into angry tears and crossed to the desk in the center of the room. "I found *this*." She showed them a cube-shaped package wrapped in plain brown paper. *End Ivan!* was written across the top of the brown paper wrapping. "This is the guest office we worked out of this week. Is it…what I think it is?"

Carly caught her breath on a wary gasp and pulled the other woman away from the desk. There was only one thing that package could be. "We need to clear the room. I need to notify the bomb squad. Let's go."

Only Ivan was moving in the other direction. *Toward* the package. He circled the desk, studying it from every direction before he grabbed the letter opener from the blotter beside the package.

"Damn it, Ivan." She watched as he pulled the paper away from the plastic-coated wires wrapped around a brick of plastic explosive. "Careful."

"It is rigged with another cell phone," Ivan announced.

Galina wept beside her. "It's like St. Feodor again. All these people…"

"Galina," Ivan chided, coming around the desk to take his chief of staff by the shoulders and gently shake her. "Pull yourself together. Do your job."

The dark-haired woman stared at him a moment before wiping away her tears and hugging her tablet to her chest. "What do you need?"

"I need you to find the ambassador. Tell him we have a situation. Have him make an announcement asking everyone to turn off their cell phones—make up some excuse about them interfering with the sound system. Then we need to calmly, without raising too much alarm, evacuate the building."

"Smoke from the kitchen," Carly suggested, rubbing Galina's back, trying to soothe her fear. "Tell them we need everyone outside on the veranda and the parking lot, so we can ventilate the building." She tilted her gaze to Ivan. "I can get to Chief Taylor. He can escort the mayor and some of the other dignitaries out."

Galina nodded. "Cell phones. Smoke. Calm evacuation. I'll have them use different exits so there's not a rush for the doors." Although it probably wasn't protocol for her to do so, she squeezed Ivan's hand before he pulled away. "You're the target, Your Highness. What about you? Shall I send Filip in here?"

"He's outside. He can help keep things organized out there."

"Danya? I haven't seen him, but—"

Carly turned to face her. "Ivan is my responsibility. I'll make sure he gets out safely."

"You don't want me to call anyone to help?"

"No." She walked the other woman out the door. "I want you to start the evacuation."

When she stepped back inside the office, Ivan was holding his glasses close to his temple, bending down to study the bomb again. "We need to get people out of this wing and evacuate the building." He pointed to the phone on the corner of the desk. "Call Joe on that landline. Bomb squad cannot come in with full gear or we'll have chaos. Someone could get trampled or have a heart attack."

Carly called Captain Hendricks and warned him about not using cell phones. She told him to put the SWAT team on alert, that she was bringing the prince out the back way through the veranda doors. She hung up and nodded to the door, expecting Ivan to follow. "Let's go."

"I am not going anywhere."

She tugged on his arm, pulling him away from the desk. "You're not staying here with this bomb."

"I can disarm it. It is not that complicated. Plastique. Wires. The cell phone is not counting down. I can disconnect it—"

"Just because you worked with explosives back in Moravska doesn't mean this is your job. You have a whole country you're responsible for. We need to close off this room and leave."

The music stopped abruptly, and, for a split second, Carly felt as though it was her heart that had stopped. Why was Ivan taking such a stupid risk? "Don't be a hero, Ivan. We have no idea when that bomb will go off."

He glanced up at the grandfather clock standing in the corner of the office. It was barely eleven o'clock. "I am guessing within the next hour. Today was the date on the picture he gave me."

The ambassador's voice coming over the sound system and the rising murmur of the guests responding to the unexpected interruption of their evening echoed the tension twisting through Carly. "Ivan, please."

Ticktock.

"Wait a minute…" Ivan slid the letter opener beneath a trio of wires and lifted them away from the plastique. "The phone is not connected to the explosive. There is no way to remotely detonate it." Blue eyes drilled into hers. "This bomb is a fake."

A fake? After all those threats? Naming the date of Ivan's death? Oh, hell. The hooded man moving through the hedge outside? A bomb inside the embassy? Guests evacuating to the parking lot? "Does that mean…?"

He was already running to the door. "There's another bomb."

They dashed down the hallway and stopped when they saw the orderly mass exodus leaving the building. Just like the scene at the Plaza, when they were being herded toward the parking garage. Toward the bomb.

"A car bomb killed Eduard," Carly said.

"They are taking them out to the parking lot," Ivan muttered at the same time.

Carly ran back to the phone. "I'll tell the captain."

Ivan hovered in the doorway. "We need to find Aleks."

"He's probably on his way outside with the others."

"We have to find him. Priority one is saving Aleks."

"Priority one is saving you." Carly hung up the phone and lifted the hem of her skirt to get to her weapon. She tugged on the lapel of Ivan's jacket and turned him so that she could enter and clear the hallway in front of him. "I have to get you to the SWAT van. That's what we agreed on."

Ivan pulled her hand away and backed into the office. "Go. Stay with Aleks. Get him someplace safe. I need to take this bomb apart."

"You said it wasn't a real bomb."

"Connect it to a trigger and it will take out this wing of the embassy. If we leave it alone, anyone could sneak in and do that."

"Then I'm staying with you."

Ivan pushed her out the door. "Save the prince!"

"But you…" Her back hit the opposite wall and she stood there long enough for confusion to segue into understanding. Then anger sent her charging across the hall. "Damn it, I knew something was off." She swatted his arm. Although, she wasn't sure if her anger was directed at him or toward herself for not guessing the truth. "You're not Prince Ivan. When I read those files… When I see the two of you together, you're so protective of him."

The man of purpose, the man of regal power and supreme confidence suddenly seemed unsure.

"Carly…" He reached for her, but she shrugged off his touch.

Her anger turned into a hurt she felt right down to her bones. "Aleksandr Petrovic?"

He nodded. "I tried to tell you the other night. When we were…in bed."

"But I didn't want to talk." She raked her fingers into her hair, knocking loose some of the upswept curls. She'd been a naive idiot. "I got so carried away."

"*We* got carried away." Ivan's hands were on her shoulders again. His sure, familiar hands. Only, they weren't Ivan's hands. "I should have tried harder. When you said you *felt* the truth about me, I thought—"

"That I knew you were fake? That you were lying

to me?" She pulled away and paced across the room. "I meant I knew what was in your heart."

"You do. I have never lied about that. Not about this chemistry between us. Not about my feelings for you." He caught her by the hand and turned her to face him. "You must have sensed something. You are too good a cop not to have at least suspected."

She nodded. She had suspected something. But she'd been so caught up in her feelings, compounded by the time limit on this affair, that she'd ignored what the clues had tried to tell her. "The scars. Losing your parents. Growing up poor. None of that happened to Ivan. That was *your* story you were sharing. You slipped up."

"Because you were so easy to talk to. You understood me. The real me. We have much in common. I have been living the lie for so long, I did not realize how much I needed someone who cared about me, not the role I was playing."

"If I could read Lukin, I would have discovered the truth. The details in Aleks's file are yours." She pulled away and lifted her skirt to reholster her gun. She didn't have to save this man. "What are you, Ivan's bodyguard? His friend?"

"Both. I am the geeky computer guy, as you say, who runs tech for the prince's security team. We have switched places before—years ago when we realized how much we look alike, covering duty shifts, going to class when one of us overslept, stupid stuff—nothing recent, and never on this grand a stage before. But after the bombing in St. Feodor—"

"You threw yourself over him when that bomb went

off. That's how you got those scars—protecting the prince. You're protecting him now."

He nodded. "We switched places seven weeks ago, as soon as the doctor cleared me to return to duty. I'd been away recuperating—it was easy enough to change our hair, our glasses."

She touched the bruise that had been dimmed by makeup on her jaw. "The doctor knew?"

"He was familiar with my injuries—and Ivan and I both thought it was prudent for him to know the truth, in case any health issues cropped up for the real prince while we traveled."

She was silent, not sure what to say. She'd given this man her heart, her body. And he'd lied.

"I did not tell you because I promised Ivan I would not. I wanted to. I wanted you to know the truth. But my sworn duty is to my future king."

"I understand duty. I understand why you lied. The more people who know who an undercover operative is, the harder it becomes to keep it a secret."

"Yes, *dorogoy*. You understand, but do you forgive me?"

Dorogoy. Darling. Did he really love her? She pressed her hands to either side of her head, wishing she could make the hurt and mistrust go away. But she couldn't. Not in this moment. Not when she wasn't even sure what *she* was feeling anymore.

She pointed to the desk. "We have bigger issues to deal with right now. I'll get Aleks…" She shook her head, clearing her thoughts to at least one thing. Duty. "I'll get Prince Ivan out to the van. You see what you can do about that bomb." She paused in the doorway and turned back to those piercing blue eyes. "Do not blow yourself up. We have more to talk about."

Then she ran to join the exiting crowd.

Chapter Twelve

His one fear had been that he would hurt her. He hadn't realized how much seeing that look of betrayal in Carly's beautiful eyes would hurt him.

Aleksandr—had he really gotten so used to thinking of himself as Ivan?—couldn't shake the sense of loss he felt when he saw Carly running away from him. But he could compartmentalize his feelings and deal with the job at hand. The military had trained him to do that. His oath to his future king demanded it.

While the grandfather clock ticked away in the corner, he searched through the desk to find tools he could use. A small pair of scissors. Tweezers. Although this explosive wasn't rigged to blow, he worried that any spark from the cell phone might set off the C-4 accidentally. That meant untangling his way through these wires and removing the phone without building up any kind of static charge as he worked.

He pulled off his glasses that did more to distort his view of the world than correct his slight astigmatism. But they'd been a necessary part of his disguise to pass as the prince, who was nearsighted. He clipped the first few wires and unwound another to pull the phone free of the explosive. Then, he pried the phone apart and removed the battery.

Crisis averted. He breathed in a sigh of momentary relief. Time to make sure the prince was safe.

In that deep breath, Aleksandr caught a whiff of faint perfume lingering in the air. Carly didn't wear perfume—she smelled like the delicious foods she cooked. This was more exotic. Was that Galina's scent? She'd been gone for nearly fifteen minutes. Shouldn't her perfume have dissipated by now?

Sniffing the air, he followed the scent to the drapes at the window and pulled them aside. The window was unlatched, hanging open a fraction of an inch. All the windows on this side of the building had the same floor-to-ceiling design as the veranda doors. Had the bomber come in this way? Or gotten out?

His gaze dropped past the excess folds of the heavy gold brocade to a swatch of dark, dusty material stashed behind the curtain. Aleksandr knelt to grasp what was clearly a sleeve. A collar. A hooded coat. He lifted the coat to his nose, breathed in the overpowering perfume and residue of sweat from a hot summer afternoon, and then he cursed.

Galina had worn this. Tonight. On the Plaza. A replica of the coat worn by the rebel bomber in St. Feodor. Her perfume was expensive and distinct.

Why? Why would the prince's chief of staff want to kill him? Galina Honchar wasn't a political rebel. She had no ties to criminal families. Aleksandr shook his head and pushed to his feet. The whys didn't matter. This was over. He knew who had murdered Eduard Nagy, who had poisoned Frank Valentine, who had tried to kill the prince.

"Carly!" She'd be out of earshot by now, but he called to her, anyway. They were a team. Together, they'd found the answers he needed. "Carly!" He whirled around to see the dark-haired woman standing in the doorway. "Galina."

She held her tablet in one hand and a gun in the other. A gun she pointed squarely at him.

"The building is clear, Your Highness." She eyed the dismantled device on top of the desk. "You took apart my little toy." She strolled toward him. She set the tablet on the corner of the desk and typed in a number on the screen. "But I have another."

He tossed the coat back into its heap, wondering if she had any kind of skill with that gun and just how badly he'd get hurt if he charged her. But more than the gun, he worried about what the numbers and the blinking prompt on her tablet meant. So he stood his ground. For now. "We know about the car bomb, Galina. KCPD and embassy security are searching for it right now."

She trailed her finger around the frame of the tablet. "Yes, but will they find it before I press this button and kill, I don't know, seven innocent people? Just like St. Feodor? Maybe more? All I have to do is send this message."

If she'd been crying earlier, there was no sign of those tears now in her cold, dark eyes. This woman was beyond feeling anything but the rage that consumed her. "You've taken apart many things that were mine. You've destroyed so much."

Aleksandr took a step forward, testing her reflexes. The gun never wavered. He put up his hands in a placating gesture, pretending that understanding made a difference. But he wasn't about to retreat. He had to get that tablet away from her. He had to get past that gun first. "This is about Konrad, the man you loved. This is all about revenge."

Galina nodded. "I simply wanted to poison you— to see you die a painful, horrible death. The Loyalists would have taken the blame for the threats and your death, and all of Lukinburg would understand the pain that I have suffered because of you. But the apples got away from me. You wanted to give them to your girl-friend. Your stupid girlfriend! After that mistake, I realized I would have to be more clever. My Konrad taught me many things. How to love. How to build a bomb. How to fire a gun. But he didn't teach me how to live without him. How to live with his senseless death. He died protecting you."

"Konrad's death is no excuse for this." He channeled every imperial syllable of the prince's tone he could. "You will kill many innocent people. Kon would not want that."

"I want that!" She stepped toward him, using the gun to direct him away from the window while she picked up the coat. "My world was perfect until you came along and started changing everything. What was wrong with the old ways? I was happy. In love. Konrad was alive." She tossed the coat onto the desk.

"That stupid reporter nearly caught me in here. Otherwise, I'd have cleaned up after myself. Just like I've always cleaned up after your messes. Everything had to be just the way His Royal Highness the Prince of Lukinburg wanted it." Aleksandr countered her position, inching closer to the tablet. She motioned him into the chair beside her and ordered him to sit. Feeling the barrel of the gun pressing against his skull gave him no choice but to oblige. "*You* made enemies, and *he* paid the price. Now you're going to pay." She circled the desk again, turning the tablet to face her. "What a tragic, humiliating end to your visit to Kansas City. You will die. Your people will die. Your regime will fail. You can't stop me."

Carly Valentine's kick-ass tone sounded from the doorway behind Galina. "I can."

The color drained from Galina's face before Aleksandr saw the flash of sparkling turquoise behind her. Galina raised both hands, including the gun, as Carly circled around her, her own gun trained on the back of Galina's head as she reached for the weapon to disarm her.

"KCPD. You are under arrest—"

He saw the grim determination flatten Galina's mouth. "Carly!"

Galina ducked and swung around, cracking the gun against Carly's arm, sending Carly's weapon flying. Galina lunged toward the desk.

"Keep her away from that tablet!" Aleksandr shot to his feet, but it really was no contest.

There was a fistful of hair, a kick to the knees and

Galina was pinned to the floor. Carly kicked one gun out of reach beside the door and twisted around to locate where her gun had landed. Galina tried to roll away from her, and she was forced to put a knee in Galina's back and hold her in place. "Really, lady? You want to keep fighting me?"

Aleksandr picked up the tablet. "Will turning this off set off the bomb?" he demanded.

"Go to hell," was Galina's answer.

"I will take that as a no." Good thing he knew a little bit about computers. He disabled the tablet's Wi-Fi connection, closed down the screen and pried open the back to remove the battery, just as he'd pulled apart the phone.

He heard footsteps running in the hallway as he set down the tablet. He was pulling off his belt to give Carly something to bind Galina's wrists with when a trio of men burst through the door. He was not a happy man. It didn't matter that Ivan was flanked by both Filip and Danya. He shouldn't be anywhere close to this traitorous witch. "What are you doing here?"

"Are you all right?" Ivan asked. "Carly?"

Filip and Danya must not know they had the real prince with them. "Get him out of here."

The two bodyguards rushed forward, pulling Aleksandr to his feet and flanking him. But Ivan wouldn't listen. "Galina Honchar, I accuse you of treason. Danya, take her into custody."

"Shut up, party boy." Galina was beyond reasoning now. "You're a waste of my time."

The prince stepped forward. "How dare you speak to your future king like that?"

"Future king?" Galina repeated.

"What?" Filip and Danya stood there agape.

Danya released Aleksandr first and moved to stand beside Ivan. "You are the prince?"

Ivan grinned. "Surprise."

Danya turned on Filip. "Did you know this?"

Filip glared at Aleksandr. "I did not."

"What are you saying?" Galina seemed more stunned than either of the men. "You? With all your sightseeing and flirting... I could have killed you a dozen times. Those nights we worked late at the hotel while he was with her?" Galina's roar of frustration was almost feral. "I will kill you!"

Carly hadn't spotted her gun yet, but Galina had. Fueled by whatever grief and anger was driving her, she twisted away from Carly and grabbed the gun from beneath the desk. She rolled, fired.

Aleksandr leaped in front of the prince and felt the bullet strike him in the chest. Pain blossomed on the right side of his rib cage as if he'd been struck by a rocket.

"No!" Carly shouted, her concern followed just as quickly by a curse. And then she switched her focus entirely and took Galina down again. She wrestled control of the gun and jammed it against Galina's neck before the woman finally stilled. "Is he hurt?"

While Filip and Ivan helped him sit up, Danya went to Carly. He picked up the discarded belt and wound it tightly around Galina's arms above her elbows. "This will hold her for now."

Carly shook her head. "She's not getting off another shot. I'm not letting go. Is he hurt?" she demanded.

"I am all right," he reassured her, breathing through the bruising pain. He unbuttoned his shirt and peeled it back to reveal the flattened bullet that had lodged in his protective vest. The shot might not have cracked a rib, but it sure did feel as if it had. He wished he could read the message in Carly's green eyes. Worry? Anger? He still reassured her. "The wind is knocked from my chest. I will be all right."

And then he turned his attention to the prince, who helped him to his feet. "What are you doing here? You're supposed to be safe in the SWAT van."

"Galina wasn't with the rest of the entourage. Neither were you. I was worried. I may be a prince, but I am also your friend. Your very grateful friend."

"Yeah, this is touching," Carly groused. "I need handcuffs." Joe Hendricks and two members of the SWAT team entered the room. She glanced up at him and saw him holding his side. "And a medic."

One of the officers immediately knelt and pulled out his cuffs to take Galina into custody. The other went to the desk to examine the explosive.

"You okay, Valentine?" Joe asked, helping Carly to her feet. That's when Aleksandr noticed that Carly had taken off her shoes—or lost them in the mud outside. "We found the second bomb in the royal limo. Bomb squad is taking it apart now."

Aleksandr moved to the desk. "This one has been

dismantled, but they will want to dispose of the components properly." He handed Joe the tablet. "Take this, too. Any good computer tech in your crime lab should be able to trace when she used it to set off the bomb that killed Eduard."

"I'll send someone in to clear the room. SWAT Team Two is doing a full sweep of the building. We'll debrief later." He nodded to the two SWAT officers. "Get her out of here." He turned to the real prince. "Your Highness. If you would kindly stay where we put you this time. It'd be a hell of a lot easier to keep you safe."

Filip agreed. "We will make sure he remains secure. Danya?"

Suddenly, the room was empty except for him and Carly. He got a glimpse of one gorgeous leg as she pulled up her dress to holster her weapon again.

She didn't seem affected by his obvious attraction to her. "You need to be checked by a medic."

When she headed for the door, he blocked her path. "We need to talk."

"Ivan... I mean, Aleksandr. Aleks? What do I call you?"

He took a deep breath. This wouldn't be easy, but he had to make this right. "My friends call me Aleks."

Her lips warped into a frown before she extended her hand to shake his. "Nice to meet you, Aleks. I'm Carly Valentine. I have issues with people who lie to me."

"And you are always honest with me." He tightened his grip and held on when she would have pulled away. "I am sorry I have hurt you. That was never my intent.

But I had to keep my word to the prince. I became him to keep him safe."

"You just took a bullet for him. Good job. You're a man of your word. May I have my hand back?"

"No." He pulled her into his arms. She put up a token fight but stopped the moment he winced at a shove against his bruised ribs. "I wanted you to love me. The man whose parents were murdered, the man who served six years in the army." He lifted her hand to his face and held it where she had touched him so many times before. "The man with the scars. Is there any way you would give Aleksandr Petrovic a second chance? One where I do not lie to you?"

The grandfather clock chimed midnight.

Carly rested her hands on his chest for a moment, then busied her fingers rebuttoning his shirt and straightening his tie. When the chimes stopped, she pulled away, as if that was her cue to leave. "You have to go back to Lukinburg. Today. We survived the deadline. Your traitor has been identified. No more bombs. You have to protect Ivan. I don't even have a passport. We'll probably never see each other again."

"Carly—"

"I'm glad for the time we had. Truly. I felt special. It felt…real."

"Aleksandr." Danya called to him from the doorway. "His Highness would like to speak to you."

"You'd better not keep your boss waiting." Carly put on a brave smile that made him feel as if he'd taken that bullet to the heart. "You said one week. You never lied about that." He retreated to the door but wasn't ready to leave her. "I knew about the time limit on this assignment. I understood I was never going to have a prince of my own—no matter how much I loved him."

Everything inside him went perfectly still, then bloomed with hope. "You love...?"

Danya grumbled a curse. "Petrovic. We must make a statement to the police and then get the prince back to our hotel."

Carly waved him away. "Go. Duty calls. We both know how that is."

Duty. How many times in his life had he chosen duty over love?

How many times had he even been given the choice?

Aleksandr cupped the side of Carly's neck and tipped her face up to cover her mouth in one last hard, passionate kiss. *"Obicham te, dorogoy."*

Then he drew his finger across her cheek and followed Danya down the hallway.

Chapter Thirteen

"Carly! Rise and shine. You have a visitor."

Carly pulled the pillow over her head to muffle the noise of her brother knocking on her bedroom door. When it didn't stop, she threw the pillow across the room and sat up. "I was up late, Frank. Fix your own breakfast for once."

"I ate three hours ago."

She glanced over at the clock. It was nearly noon. Maybe he was looking for lunch. She didn't have much of an appetite herself. Possibly because she was still full of the pint of coffee ice cream she'd eaten when she'd gotten home from the ball. Or maybe because after that self-pity pig-out, she'd cried in the shower until the water had run cold. Then she'd put on her sweats and had run a couple of miles around the neighborhood to clear her head, falling into bed as the sun was coming up. She might have a better grasp on everything that had happened this past week—she might even have a sense of acceptance over the way things had ended with Ivan, no, make that Aleksandr. But she was still too emotionally drained and exhausted to be hungry.

Or social.

Or nice to her brother.

"Go away, Frank!"

"No can do, Carly Barley. It's official police business. He says he needs to talk to Officer Valentine."

Carly tipped her head back and groaned. "Give me five minutes to get presentable."

"Okeydoke."

She was out of bed and freshening up in the bathroom before she heard him head back upstairs. The stack of condoms she'd stolen from Jesse's old room sat on the counter beside the sink, taunting her. Before the memory of that special night overtook her and left her sobbing again, she opened a drawer and dumped them inside. She pulled on a pair of cutoffs and tank top, twisted her hair into a braid and hurried up the stairs, barefoot.

"Who is it, Frank? I'm on vaca..."

"I brought you a present." She froze at the deep, accented voice she found so sexy. Aleksandr Petrovic, once known as His Royal Highness Prince Ivan of Lukinburg, handed her a large, rectangular box with a turquoise ribbon tied around it. He set it in her hands and she nearly dropped it, partly because of the unexpected weight, and partly because she was in shock at seeing him here. He caught the box before it hit the floor and held it out to her again. "I see that you can use a pair of shoes."

Carly couldn't look away from those blue eyes.

"What are you doing here? Aren't you supposed to be on a flight to Lukinburg right now? It'll be a long walk home."

"Perhaps not."

"Okay, a long swim."

"I am staying in Kansas City."

Carly blinked. He was staying? She blinked again. "But…" She dropped the box to the floor and closed the distance between them, wrapping her arms around his waist and snuggling in to the place she liked best. "I'm sorry."

His arms folded around her and he whispered against her hair. "For what, *dorogoy*?"

"For getting stuck in my head and not listening to my heart. I felt stupid that I hadn't seen your deception. But then I realized you had to be really good at your job to pull that off, and I admire you for that. You said we would fake a relationship, but every bit of it was real except for your name. I didn't want you to go last night. I don't want you to go now. Wait. Why are you staying?" She pushed against him to see into his eyes and immediately apologized when he grimaced in pain.

"You're hurt?"

"Some bruising and swelling. The doctor says I will be fine."

"Carls, my dear." Her father had gotten off the sofa to join them in the foyer. "The guy's been wounded in action. Ask him in for coffee. Frank? Let's go out back and inspect that work you've been doin' on my deck." He reached out to shake Aleks's hand. "You know she's got two big brothers and me lookin' out for her if you don't treat her right."

"Dad!"

But Aleks grinned. "I would be more scared of her than any of you if I screw this up."

Her father laughed. "Then you do know her. You're okay, Mr. Prince. I like you." He ended the handshake to hug Carly to his side. "Is this what you want?"

She hugged him back. "*He's* what I want."

He kissed the top of her head. "Then go for it. We'll give you two some privacy."

"Thanks, Dad."

Several minutes later, Carly was wearing the burgundy boots she'd admired when she'd been shopping for evening gowns, and she was sitting in Aleks's lap on the couch. "They're beautiful. I love them." She gave him a quick kiss. "Thank you."

Aleks wore another suit and crisp white shirt, but this time without the tie. He looked downright casual and infinitely handsome. He skimmed his hand up and down her leg, from the cuff of her shorts to the top of her new boots and back. The friction of his gentle caress warmed her skin and heated things up deeper inside. "I did not think you would like another pair of those sparkly heels. These make you smile."

"You make me smile." She stroked the fine silk of his beard along his jaw. "You're sure you aren't in any danger from Galina Honchar? Or Lukin rebels? I'd rather not play bodyguard again if I don't have to."

"Galina is being extradited to Lukinburg where she will stand trial. Danya…" Carly tightened her fingers against his skin when he hesitated. "He was not happy to have his brother's death be the excuse she used to assassinate the prince. He is taking some time off. But I advised Ivan to ask him to take over as security chief, and encourage Filip to retire."

"Sounds like a smart plan," Carly agreed. "Now tell me again why you're not going home to St. Feodor with Ivan?"

He pressed a kiss into her palm and smiled. "I asked to be assigned to Kansas City to represent Lukinburg's interests here. There may be a time when I go back to my country. For a visit. But by then, you will have a passport. There is much I would like to show you, just as I have seen much of your beautiful city." He nuzzled the shell of her ear, then kissed his way down her neck until he found the bundle of nerves that made her squiggle in his lap. He smiled against her skin as it heated beneath his touch. "I cannot make you a princess, but perhaps you would be content to be a geeky computer nerd's wife."

"I already said yes." Carly captured his jaw between her hands and kissed him again. "Do you really love me?"

"That is what *obicham te* means."

The guttural expression of his feelings warmed her as thoroughly as his touch. "I want to learn more of your language."

"I will teach you."

"Will you take me dancing?"

"Every night if you wish." He smiled. "Since we are laying down the ground rules of this very real relationship, I know that you wish to continue your work with

KCPD. They are very lucky to have you. But you will still have time to bake me a pie?"

"What flavor would you like?"

His smile faded, but the intensity of those blue eyes never dimmed. "Will you love me for who I really am?"

"Aleksandr Petrovic—I didn't fall in love with a prince. I fell in love with a man." She traced the scar that cut through his beard and then touched her lips to the brave, vulnerable spot. "I fell in love with *you*."

* * * * *

Look for more books from USA TODAY *bestselling author Julie Miller coming soon.*

And don't miss these previous books from Julie Miller:

Kansas City Cop
Rescued by the Marine
Do-or-Die Bridesmaid

Available now from Harlequin Intrigue!

INTRIGUE

Available August 20, 2019

#1875 TANGLED THREAT
by Heather Graham
Years ago, FBI agent Brock McGovern was arrested for a crime he didn't commit. Now that he's been cleared of all charges, he'll do whatever it takes to find the culprit. With two women missing, Brock's ex-girlfriend Maura Antrium is eager to help him. Can they find the killer...or will he find them first?

#1876 FULL FORCE
Declan's Defenders • by Elle James
After working at the Russian embassy in Washington, DC, Emily Chastain is targeted by a relentless killer. When she calls upon Declan's Defenders in order to find someone to help her, former Force Recon marine Frank "Mustang" Ford vows to find the person who is threatening her.

#1877 THE SAFEST LIES
A Winchester, Tennessee Thriller • by Debra Webb
Special Agent Sadie Buchanen is deep in the backcountry of Winchester, Tennessee, in order to retrieve a hostage taken by a group of extreme survivalists. When she finds herself in danger, she must rely on Smith Flynn, an intriguing stranger who is secretly an undercover ATF special agent.

#1878 MURDERED IN CONARD COUNTY
Conard County: The Next Generation • by Rachel Lee
When a man is killed, Blaire Afton and Gus Maddox, two park rangers, must team up to find the murderer. Suddenly, they discover they are after a serial killer... But can they stop him before he claims another victim?

#1879 CONSTANT RISK
The Risk Series: A Bree and Tanner Thriller • by Janie Crouch
A serial killer is loose in Dallas, and only Bree Daniels and Tanner Dempsey can stop him. With bodies piling up around them, can they find the murderer before more women die?

#1880 WANTED BY THE MARSHAL
American Armor • by Ryshia Kennie
After nurse Kiera Connell is abducted by a serial killer and barely escapes with her life, she must rely on US marshal Travis Johnson's protection. But while Travis believes the murderer is in jail, Kiera knows a second criminal is on the loose and eager to silence her.

YOU CAN FIND MORE INFORMATION ON UPCOMING HARLEQUIN® TITLES, FREE EXCERPTS AND MORE AT WWW.HARLEQUIN.COM.

HICNM0819

Get 4 FREE REWARDS!

We'll send you 2 FREE Books plus 2 FREE Mystery Gifts.

Harlequin Intrigue* books feature heroes and heroines that confront and survive danger while finding themselves irresistibly drawn to one another.

FREE Value Over **$20**

SPECIAL EXCERPT FROM

◆ **HARLEQUIN**®
™
I N T R I G U E

It's been years since Brock McGovern was last in his hometown—the place where he was once accused of a crime he did not commit. Now, with the help of his high school sweetheart, Maura Antrim, he's investigating another murder... But can they find a criminal who has always remained in the shadows?

Read on for a sneak preview of
Tangled Threat,
by New York Times *bestselling author Heather Graham.*

"I've been assigned to go back to Florida. To stay at the Frampton Ranch and Resort—and investigate what we believe to be three kidnappings and a murder. And the kidnappings may have nothing to do with the resort, nor may the murder?" Brock McGovern asked, a small note of incredulity slipping into his voice, which was surprising to him—he was always careful to keep an even tone.

FBI assistant director Richard Egan had brought him into his office, and Brock had known he was going on assignment—he just hadn't expected this.

"Yes, not what you'd want, but, hey, maybe it'll be good for you—and perhaps necessary now, when time is of the essence and there is no one out there who could know the place or the circumstances with the same scope and experience you have," Egan told him. "Three young women have disappeared from the area. Two of them were guests of the Frampton Ranch and Resort shortly before their disappearances—the third had left St. Augustine and was on her way there. The Florida Department of Law Enforcement has naturally been there already. They asked for federal help on this. Shades of the past haunt them—they don't want any more unsolved murders—and everyone is hoping against hope that Lily Sylvester, Amy Bonham and Lydia Merkel might be found."

"These are Florida missing-person cases," Brock said. "And it's sad but true that young people go to Florida and get caught up in the beach life and the club scene. And regrettable but true once again—there's a drug and alcohol culture that does exist and people get caught up in it. Not just in Florida, of course, but everywhere." He smiled grimly. "I go where I'm told, but I'm curious—how is this an FBI affair? And forgive me, but—FBI out of New York?"

"Not out of New York. FDLE asked for you. Specifically."

Don't miss
Tangled Threat *by Heather Graham,*
available September 2019 wherever
Harlequin® books and ebooks are sold.

www.Harlequin.com

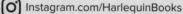